To Nalini

from

Tom X

(the Author !!!☆)

Jan 2020

Voices from a Wendy House Contrivance

A Drama Novel

TOM WALTERS

authorHOUSE®

AuthorHouse™ UK
1663 Liberty Drive
Bloomington, IN 47403 USA
www.authorhouse.co.uk
Phone: 0800.197.4150

Published by AuthorHouse 06/27/2019

ISBN: 978-1-7283-8214-2 (sc)
ISBN: 978-1-7283-8215-9 (e)

Print information available on the last page.

Any people depicted in stock imagery provided by Getty Images are
models, and such images are being used for illustrative purposes only.
Certain stock imagery © Getty Images.

This book is printed on acid-free paper.

'VOICES FROM A WENDY HOUSE CONTRIVANCE'

Sometimes late at night! Sometimes in the wee small hours in the morning! I hear voices. They tell me how it is for them, they question, they plead, they laugh, they cry, they justify, they deny, they love, they hate –they live. My voice is there too –part of the choir. Their refrain is my refrain. Their lyrics are timeless but their voices are transient, they rise and they fall and they are forever trapped, we are forever trapped, in a 'Wendy House' world and in trying to find our way out............

CONTENTS

INTERLUDE 1
An Impudent and Mendacious Interruption!

I SHOULD HAVE WRITTEN THIS. YES, REALLY —OH BY the way let me introduce myself. My name is John Julian Childs, Deputy Head of Belle View Primary School...You'll find out something about me in due course. Yes, I'm in the story, grossly caricatured of course but recognisable..Walter wrote this..Walter Sidebrother, one of our junior teachers here. He's in it too. Didn't think he had it in him. Mind if I smoke?......I always thought Walter was your sensitive, interpretative <u>artiste</u> as opposed to your macho, creative artist...You know, the village idiot who makes everyone laugh and is a helpful, useful scapegoat in any sort of ingrown neurotic community like a school... Quite surprised me!.....<u>I</u> could have written this. Mind you, it would have been much more hard-headedly realistic not so infantile in conception, more subtle –it would certainly not have been a sit com –school life is a bloody tragedy, any teacher can tell you that! I would have called it 'The Wendy House' –you know, shades of Ibsen. It would have been a play to start with, and not a sad little story, <u>and</u> much more tightly structured in both design and intent....I would have been the tragic hero of course...Shot by the Head in the act of giving some poor bastard a free period! ..Shot <u>by</u> the Head <u>in</u> the head, so perish all teachers, collapsing before the blackboard leaving a trail of chalk and a crowd of unsympathetic children asking if they still had to do the homework I set them! Inevitably the whole thing would have been a flop. That's why I never wrote it....Not that there's much to Walter's story. It's got a loose and flabby overall structure rather reminiscent of those seedy sideshows you get in the poorer travelling fairs, all stuck together with poles and bits of rope and striped canvas...inconsequential ....that's why he calls it 'Voices From A Wendy House Contrivance'... clever that though, admitting his fault before he starts.....''

"I never started at all, perhaps I should have done. Anyway, take a look at it....See what you think. Don't judge us too harshly, remember it's a gross caricature of everyone... Walter may not be a Shakespeare but he is a persistent little buggar and some of it may get to you if you're not too careful and you may think you know more than you do .."

First Staff Meeting – Autumn Term

As each member of staff enters the staffroom there should be a commentary/voice-over in a quiet, dignified BBC style as used when introducing famous people at a royal reception.

Howard Bulcastle enters. Shabbily dressed, greasy tie, collar pointing up, uncombed hair. He carries a bundle of papers and makes for the staffroom table to sort them out somewhat chaotically.

Howard Bulcastle, aged 61, red-headed, glisteningly-bulbous-nosed Head of Belle View Primary school. A large, dominating, inarticulate man – A lover of all sports and would-be appreciator of the arts –thinks ballet is 'gymnastics to music' –Given to telling rambling unfunny stories about his wartime experiences in the R.A.F. as bomb aimer.

John Julian creeps in. He looks weary, doesn't greet Bulcastle. Goes over to the sink to make a cup of coffee and stands staring out of the window.

John Julian Childs, aged 55, Deputy Head and in charge of Music and Arts. A grey-bearded devotee of the arts –wears wine-coloured velvet dinner jackets and 'hush puppies'. Prefers teaching to 'education' and thinks that even this is no substitute for happiness. Smokes a lot and chases younger members of staff in his free periods.

Perdita O'Toole enters. She goes straight over to greet

Bulcastle enthusiastically. He looks vaguely embarrassed and continues working on his papers. She goes over to greet Childs and then proceeds to make tea/coffee for all the rest as they enter.

Perdita O'Toole (aged 54), Head of Infant Department. Soft-spoken with a Southern Irish lilt. Spends her breaktimes knitting woollens for refugees and making snide remarks about the Head Teacher and the Caretaker. Strongly dissociates herself from the I.R.A. and has framed portraits at home of the Pope and the Archbishop of Limerick, as well as the leader of her local Tory-controlled council. Hates blood sports but keeps her brother's shillelagh under her bed at night.

Brenda Gratten bursts in. Looks nervously to the left and to the right, then sits awkwardly on the edge of her seat in the middle of the room and stares into space, smoking and inhaling deeply.

Brenda Gratten, (aged 44), Senior Mistress –Head of P.E. and Girls' games. Married to a much older invalid husband who is an extremely wealthy stockbroker. Spends her evenings playing squash when she isn't studying her insurance policies –a loud rasping voice and a tendency to explode into hysterical spasms of cackling laughter on any topic that may have a possible sexual innuendo. She chain –smokes and is planning a hysterectomy later in the year. Strikes fear in the children and awe amongst the staff.

Avis Gunn rushes in as though she is late. She doesn't greet anyone but spends her time searching the staffroom from top to bottom for something she has mislaid.

Avis Gunn (aged 38) –Towsled haired, slightly dotty, 'dedicated' teacher –Often up till two in the morning making workcards or marking books –Always losing things and spends her time walking round in circles in quick little steps –Speaks like the 'Infant teacher' she is –but the 'Teacher of the Year' Award is hers for the taking.

Radcliffe Ball saunters in. Very popular, she greets everyone in turn and they greet her. She is aging but has a young face and dresses youthfully-A Hampstead/blue-stocking manner but 'homely' with it.

Radcliffe Ball (aged 55) Nature-loving 'Top Junior' teacher. Her classroom is a jungle of books, apparatus, art work, animals, plants, children-Completely absent-minded about whose hall period it is but remembers everybody's birthday and all the children's first names.

Walter Sidebrother enters boldly –extends his arms in mock acknowledgement of recognition and applause. Nobody takes any notice and he makes his own coffee. He winks at the reader in sly complicity.

Just a moment, that's me! Good God! Nervous, bespectacled Top Junior teacher with a great mop of curly hair that makes him look ridiculously younger than he actually is, 35. Surviving his second nervous breakdown and looking forward to his third –Missed his vocation, should have been a clown like his famous sister –Instead he entertains the staff and 'kids' in slapstick style when he is not intimidating them with his formidably esoteric and useless knowledge.

Allison Prestatyn sheepishly sidles in. Peers at everyone over her gold-rimmed specs, looks vaguely surprised, drops her books. Bulcastle chivalrously rushes over to pick them up. Childs lustfully rushes over with a coffee (milk and no sugar). Sidebrother minces after her as she finds a seat. Brenda draws on her ciggie and looks on in half-amused disgust.

Allison Prestatyn (aged 23), a new teacher ('spanking new', thinks John Julian), who creates chaos in her Reception

Class when she arrives, apologetically late, every morning. The children spend the whole day mispronouncing her name in chorus - Quite attractive, if somewhat shortsighted, and it is rumoured that her free periods are used for purposes that were never intended by Barnside Education Authority.

Enter Brunhilde Waizmann carrying a further pile of papers to Bulcastle –She enters with great dignity and aplomb –Faint strains of the 'Ride of the Valkyries' should he heard in the background.

Brunhilde Waizmann, aged 50, school secretary –sensitive to the point of suicide about her age –Looks like the Brunhilde she's named after. She comes from a distinguished and wealthy family from whom she has gained her formidably articulate mouth and overbearing self-confidence. Once at major school function, a child presented the bouquet of flowers to her instead of the Mayoress. Once at a school Sports Day she arrived like the Queen of Sheba, wearing an imperious broad-rimmed hat and accompanied by her pekinese 'Pooch' who unceremoniously widdled over Howard Bulcastle's jacket which he had carelessly left over a chair at the start of the egg and spoon race.

Bob Dredge barges in with the post. He gives the letters out with a slightly officious, grudging air. Walter takes his, sniffs it as though perfumed and then bourgeois-gentihomme-style kisses Bob's outstretched hand. Bob, crimson with embarrassment, marches out.

Bob Dredge, aged 29, school caretaker. Bullish in appearance but a bit thick. When he is not in the local pub. 'The Belle View Arms', he is finding an excuse to mend Allison's Wendy House or having a quick packet of fags in the boiler room. A keen union man –As Health & Safety Officer, he is always on the lookout for new hazards to complain about.

Hilary Trumble bustles in noisily with a large rocking

horse which she puts in the most inconvenient place in the staffroom, for Mr Childs to move. She shouts brassily, "Morning all! Hope you've had a good holiday!" To which everyone is programmed to respond, "Yes thank you Hilary!"

Hilary Trumble (aged 28) –A big girl is Hilary. Recently married and always talking about 'Desmond'. Desmond says this or Desmond says that. She's an accomplished musician who thunders out Bach's 'Chromatic Fantasy and Fugue' before the Infant Assembly can settle for 'All Things Bright and Beautiful'.

Mrs Teasdale enters with the aid of a stick and is ushered to her seat by Miss O'Toole and Mrs Gratten. She declines coffee/tea and immediately settles into the knitting which she will be doing until the end of the story or the end of time, whichever comes first.

Mrs Teasdale (Aged 65 –almost) –Large, arthritic and blessedly near retirement. Always complaining of feeling tired –A great knitter like Perdita O'Toole, but holding opposed primly protestant views. Only Mr Bulcastle and Mr Childs call her by her first name –'Betty'. Her full name Elizabeth is known only to God.

GERBILS AND TOILETS

Staff gradually drift over to form a semi-circle round the central coffee table on which Bulkcastle has still not sorted his papers –several of which have floated to the floor. He opens the meeting:-

"Right! Erhm! Hope you all had a happy and restful summer holiday. Your timetables are on your desks or should be on your desks erhm! First things first though.

Mrs Teasdale's hamster is still missing since last term. Mr Dredge has seen it on a number of occasions, so if you could just keep a weather eye open.....

"God!!" Brenda rumbles, smoking and inhaling deeply!

Mrs Teasdale looks daggers at the blasphemer but pointedly ignores it in her interjection, "Oh no, no, no Mr Bulcastle! It was a gerbil and its cage door was deliberately left open! I want something done about it!"

"Well..gerbil, hamster, what's the difference? We know what we're looking for anyway.."

Radcliffe adds her academic tuppenneth, "There is a difference you know Mr Bulcastle, and if we're to ask the children to look for it we've got to be able to tell them exactly what we're looking for. We mustn't pretend it doesn't matter what it's called. Isn't this what education is all about? Calling things by their right names?"

"If it gets under my feet, I know what I shall call it. Let's get on to more important matters. Toilets!"

"God!!" Brenda rumbles again, inhaling deeply.

John Julian can't resist this one: "Is that a statement of belief Brenda or an expression of disgust? I can't quite make out from your tone of voice."

Brenda finally erupts, "When am I going to get a clean classroom Mr Bulcastle, that's what I would like to know!? If you want to to know how that blessed gerbil has survived the summer holidays, it's been living off the cabbages growing on my classroom floor!!" She cackles at her own preposterousness.

There is a shocked silence at first after this neurotic outburst, broken only by the quietly, pleading voice of Avis Gunn, going off on one of her tangents: "I was wondering Mr Bulcastle when I could have that Nature Tray you promised me last term —I did ask for it on a number of occasions and you said you'd let me have it first thing!"

Howard finally loses his cool and he is at his joyously most inarticulate:

"Look! Please! We're on toilets at the moment! (Brenda cackles) We'll deal with stock later. Please! Calm down Mrs Gratten! Let's just be serious for a moment. The toilets were in a terrible state last term, as everybody here knows, and if it carries on like that this term I shall close them down! They'll just have to wait all morning and go to the outside ones at lunchtime."

Perdita, not pausing from her knitting and not looking up:

"Don't be ridiculous! You can't stop the little ones going to the toilet Mr Bulcastle, they have a way of taking the law into their own hands!"

"It would appear that's what they are doing already, Perdita. That's why the toilets are in such a state!" John Julian reasonably rejoinders.

Walter enthusiastically but nervously added his own wisdom to the matter:

"M-May I suggest that we ration the number of times they are allowed to go to the l-loo in one day, and, if they exceed their quota, as it were, we d-dock Team Points!"

Brenda pounces, "Don't be such a cretin Walter. Children don't wee wee to order or my classroom would be flooded by the end of the morning!"

"Perhaps Walter has a point!" muses John Julian sympathetically.

"Yes, the top of his head!!" Brenda lambasts mercilessly whilst at the same time unleashing within herself a current of hysterical giggles.

The staff are by this time getting a little fedup of

Brenda's rude outbursts and so John Julian attempts to calm the waters.

"Now come on Brenda! We want a nice peaceful term this time with Christmas at the end of it! May I suggest that we have 'Toilet Monitors' to control the situation at lunchtimes and breaktimes and try to prevent abuse of the system, as it were; and that we try to cut down the number of visits during lesson time."

But Brenda isn't going to let John Julian put her down as there are a lot of personal 'old scores' to settle.

"Oh that sounds fine in theory! But you don't know what first year juniors are like Mr Childs! Since, as non-teaching Deputy Head, you've not had the privilege of taking a class for the last five years!!"

The staff groan and Howard Bulcastle intervenes:

"Look, this sort of abuse is not getting us anywhere. We've got a lot of business to get through so let's press ahead!"

"But what are we going to do with the toilets?" Brenda flounders and John Julian is happy to give her the coup de grace:

"Use them my dear Brenda! Use them!"

Bulcastle settles it, "I think Mr Childs' suggestion seems eminently sensible to me. If no one has any objections… (Brenda wasn't going to push her luck)…We'll give it a go!"

"Bearing in mind that Infant needs are more pressing than junior needs!" Avis adds archly, to defuse any last remaining tensions.

Bulcastle continues with the agenda:

"Now some important dates for the term…P.C. Custard is coming on October 11th to give a talk on the 'Danger Stranger' to the Lower Juniors and Top Infants."

Mrs Teasdale mounts her hobby horse!

"May I be so bold as to ask who the danger stranger is?"

Howard Bulcastle was happy to hold the reins!

"You may well ask Betty. It could be you or I? Your average raving maniac is very often a happily married man with a steady job and three lovely children."

"I know the feeling! I know the feeling!" interjects John Julian.

Walter needs clarification!

"But surely isn't this going to make the children unduly suspicious of strangers, or anybody come to that. Uncle B-Bob offers little M-Mary a sweet and immediately she thinks he's going to have his wicked way with her!"

Brenda rises to it, "No one offers me sweets, not even you Walter!"

"I may be a stranger love but I'm not dangerous enough for you," Walter wittily ripostes.

Perdita from the lofty heights of her knitting needles settles the moral dilemma: "I think it's very important that children should be told that there are some nasty people about who will do them harm if they are given the opportunity!"

Mrs Teasdale concurs, "Hear! Hear! They want the birch! All of them!"

"They may want the birch Betty, but is it going to do them any good –or society for that matter?" says John Julian, gently prodding the hobby horse.

Mrs Teasdale is visibly rattled, "With respect Mr Childs you are much too permissive in these matters. Supposing someone assaulted your daughter! Would you be soft on the offender then? But then you're not married and you haven't any children!!"

"But I do have a vested interest in the human race Betty!" triumphs John Julian just as Howard Bulcastle rises to move the discussion on:

"We're going off the point again. So P.C Custard is coming on the 11th. Phyllis Rowbottom's 'Bring and Buy' Sale is on the 14th and we've got our Harvest Festival on the 20th. Colonel Martindale and his wife from the Salvation Army will be officiating as usual."

Avis Gunn flutters in, "Oh I was wondering Miss O'Toole if we could have 'Glad That I Live Am I', the children sing it so beautifully!"

Perdita shoots the bird down, "I was under the impression Miss Gunn that we had already decided on 'All Things Bright And Beautiful'. It's much more apposite to the occasion!"

Hilary bounces in, 'Glad That I Live Am I' is out –We haven't got the music!"

Avis is a wounded and agitated bird, "You had it last year Hilary! I turned the pages for you!"

At this auspicious moment a talking cuckoo clock bursts into song from one of the cupboards behind: "Cuckoo one o'clock! Cuckoo two o'clock!" it trills on till twelve and then starts all over again, until, that is, Howard Bulcastle's mighty Head teacher's foot against the half open door puts a timely end to its life.

Avis's half-stifles a cry of recognition, "That's my 'Talking Cuckoo Clock' for my remedial under-six maths group! I've been looking for it for absolutely ages!!"

She trots along to the cupboard to retrieve it. Takes it out, holds it out at arm's length and head cocked on one side, smiles at it until it finishes chiming.. 'There! It works perfectly, your kick didn't quite depatch it Mr Bulcastle!!"

Howard Bulcastle explodes, "Will you please stop it Miss Gunn! In case it has escaped your notice, we have an agenda to finish!"

"It doesn't matter about that Nature Tray Mr Bulcastle! At last I've found my cuckoo clock!"

"And 'cuckoo' to you too dear!" Brenda cackles.

"Avis you're always losing something!" John Julian adds.

"Except the one thing worth losing!" dejects Hilary sotto voce.

"Desmond NOT been bothering you again Hilary?" Walter notices.

"Let's get on. Please don't tell the children too early about the Harvest Festival. You'll remember that the fruit virtually walked to Barnfield Old People's Home by itself. Mrs Brigginthorpe's apple crumble was eaten by the football team and nobody knows what happened to the shewbread or the boxes of chocolates donated by Stephenson's."

Radcliffe reminisces, "I caught Boris Hancock with his pockets stuffed with olives. It is not as though he knew what they were. I think he thought they were sweets –but he <u>did</u> know that they came from Greece, which is something!"

Brenda's irritation surfaces again, "That's typical of you Radcliffe! You turn petty theft into an educational experience. If you'd wanted to bring Geography into it, you could have told him that if you steal olives in Saudi Arabia you have your hands cut off!"

John Julian seizes the opportunity, "I always wondered why the children in your class had such poor handwriting Brenda! Now I know."

"Well, that more or less brings us up to half-term. We will of course have another meeting, after half-term in November sometime, to discuss the Christmas arrangements. Now, the Rev. Fetchley Arthur Warmpit, the minister of Domesodden Christian Mission, has brought to my attention, a competition he is organising amongst schoolchildren in Barnside. The idea is that children should write a letter to God on any topic they like. The closing date for entries is October 31st."

Brenda, inhales deeply, "My God! What next! What a topic 'God'!"

"Well, the name is familiar, but the address escapes me I'm afraid!!" agrees John Julian.

"It says here (Howard reads) The children are to send their letters to 'God', c/o Rev. Fetchley Arthur Warmpit, Domesodden Christian Mission, Dewsbond St, Barnside, Middx., and they should be marked 'Competition'. Does that answer your question Mr Childs?"

"In a literal sort of way I suppose. I was wondering where God lived that's all. Silly old me should know better at my age!"

Mrs Teasdale crusades, "It's all very well to mock God and religion Mr Childs. One day the reckoning will come and the Bible says we will all be cast in a pit and only the pure will escape the flames!"

"Nasty!" deftly engages John Julian.

"The true of heart have nothing to fear, so says the Rev. Warmpit."

"And he should know!"

Brenda gives full vent, "Can't stand that self-righteous old fool! He always shoves his opinions down the kids' throats and then addresses us teachers as though we were little kids ourselves!"

Howard pacifies, "Speaking personally, I think he does a good job."

Perdita interjects above the clicking of her needles, "I don't know why we don't invite Mother Mary Paul from St Agnes –She's got a lovely way with the children.

At this point Brunhilde Waizman bursts in with

a message from on high (echoes from 'The Ride of the Valkyries'):

"Sorry to interrupt Mr Bulcastle but we've just had a message from the office –Mr Peasanthwartes himself. They want to know how many Japs we have on roll ..and I can't find your keys to the small cabinet."

"Tell him I'm in the middle of a staff meeting and I'll get back to him later."

She peremptorily replies, "But Mr Bulcastle, he told me he must know <u>now</u> what the Jap numbers are, its's very urgent. Something do with falling rolls in Barnside!"

"Just a moment!!" Howard searches vainly through his pile of papers, giving time for John Julian's bon mots:

"Brunhilde, by 'Japs' I presume you are referring to the Japanese children we have. 'Japs' is such an unfortunate appellation. It smacks of Pearl Harbour, Banzai and suicide pilots. Whereas the term 'Japanese' suggests Toyota, Mitsubishi and Datsun, not to speak of Sony, Sanyo etc etc.. On second thoughts I think that 'Japs' is marginally better."

Allison pipes up, "I asked one of my Japanese parents what part of Japan her family came from and she said Hiroshima! I felt so awful!"

Brenda bristles, "My Uncle Peter was crippled on the Burma Rd! I can't stand the Japs to put it mildly! Still I haven't got any in my class!"

Howard, red-faced and hot under the collar, gives up the search:

"You'll just have to tell him to wait Miss Waizmann because I intend to finish this meeting!"

"Very well Mr Bulcastle!" Brunhilde, slightly affronted, sails out.

Radcliffe reminisces again, "I knew a Japanese chap once – a long time ago now of course. He was a scientist attached to the Ministry of Agriculture. He was a charming man. He went back to Kyoto at the end of the war. If he'd stayed, who knows, we might eventually have got married. I've got two Japanese children in my class. They're <u>very</u> hard-working <u>and</u> polite."

Mrs Teasdale, from behind frowning spectacles and agitated knitting:

"They did some awful things to our men during the war!!"

John Julian smoulders, "What's that supposed to mean? –The war ended almost forty years ago!!"

At this point the firebell starts ringing. Lights start to flash, it goes darker. Windows and doors start to rattle and a wind can be heard accompanied by the roar of a huge distant explosion. A brilliant dazzling flash of light comes through the staffroom window and simultaneously a huge mushroom cloud can be seen rising. But no one takes any notice except for poor Walter Sidebrother.

Walter panicking, "Heavens! We're b-being invaded! It's the end of the w-world!"

Howard Bulcastle takes charge:

"Calm down Walter, it's only the firebell! Could be a false alarm but we can't take any chances so everyone out into the playground and line your classes up under the shed in the small yard! Oh one final thing! Stock may be collected from Mrs Waizmann's office, but please bring your stock books!"

Hilary shouts over-joyfully, "Before or after we are incinerated Mr Bulcastle?!"

They all rush out leaving John Julian Childs ruminating on the holocaust to come.

He walks over to the staffroom window and stares out. He lights a cigarette.

"Light my own little fire!....Well! If the school is going up in flames, it's not before time. With the amount of hot air generated in this staffroom, it's a wonder it didn't go up years ago.....I've been here far too long...Too late now....Can't escape...It's in my blood....I'm part of the furniture, as they say. When it goes, I go! But it won't go! What's actually happened is that Percy Horsfall, in Brenda's class, has pushed the fire button for a dare –I overheard him planning it in the dining hall..When you get to my age they think you're deaf aswell as stupid! I don't know what Brenda will do when she finds out. It's capital punishment for spelling mistakes in her class."

An excited Bob Dredge rushes in, where teachers fear to tread:

"We've found it! Mr Childs sir, we've found it!

"Mr Dredge, what have you found?"

"Mrs Teasdale's gerbil!"

"Mr Dredge, can you hear the firebell? The school could be burning down! Shouldn't you be putting water on it or something? On second thoughts forget it! Just tell me the good news. Who found Mrs Teasdale's gerbil?"

"It was Percy Horsfall. He said he found it near the Junior Firebell!"

"Well glory be!"

With perfect timing, Avis's Talking Cuckoo Clock starts up again!

INTERLUDE 2

ANOTHER SLIGHTLY MORE TRUTHFUL INTERRUPTION!

"**Y**ES, IT'S YOURS TRULY, JOHN JULIAN CHILDS again.....Oh he's right there! I've been here much too long. But don't get me wrong –Walter makes me out to be some kind of pathetic figure trapped in a deadend teaching job who is desperately trying to find a way out and in the end.....well, I won't give away the plot. But I'm not ending up like him, I can assure you. I've got plans in quite a different direction. Tell you more later...Mind if I smoke?...Oh it's the fire you're worried about? The nuclear holocaust??..That's just Walter's pathetic attempt to inject a bit of life into his story! Funny how major tragedies can take our minds off the real horrors of life! Nuclear holocaust indeed!....Mind you, we had a real fire once, oh yes. That was the first time Brenda and I got together. The office gave us all the afternoon off and it was a nice spring day so we decided to have a nice pub lunch down by the river....Notice the word 'nice', that's what it was.

Not exactly innocent but 'nice', at first. But it wasn't long before we got together to draft the new science syllabus at my cottage. I hasten to add there was more getting together than drafting!.....Brenda doesn't waste much time with the preliminaries I can tell you. I have never known anyone put so much fervent evangelical zeal into fucking quite like she could. I say 'could'. It all fizzzled out after a couple of terms. I was a twitching, limp, failure by the end of the school journey-Never mix education and pleasure, a fatal mistake which put paid to our relationship...Anyway, her husband was beginning to smell a rat and I loathe scenes so the end of the summer term provided a natural excuse to end the affair....She never forgave me for it, 'hell hath no fury' etc.... Put it this way, she didn't take it very well....Not that I was the first you understand. She had had a tortuous affair with Howard Bulcastle, the end of which became obvious during a heated staffroom discussion on 'Nature Trails' of all things. Their acrimoniuous exchanges revealed a lot more about the tangled path of their dreary relationship than about the tangled trail of woodland flowers....Then there was the deputy Education Officer, and even young Bob Dredge had had a go at her one cold February morning behind the pipes in the boiler room –at the time she had complained of feeling cold in the classroom and went down to see what Bob could do about it, Bob obliged!.... I ask you!... She got quite nasty towards me in the months that followed –Some of it comes out in this story – but Walter makes our relationship out to be a lot nicer and more interesting than it really was. She wrote these awful 'poison pen' letters for a long time.....a strange mixture of threats, pleadings and insults, as such letters tend to be. Then she resorted to loud. barbed conversations in the staffroom and the usual bitter exchanges at staff meetings, which had worked to such good effect with Howard.

BRENDA'S INTERRUPTION OF THE INTERRUPTION!

"Oh no you don't, you bastard! I'm not letting you get away with that nasty bit of self-righteousness, You think you're in command of things, don't you? A right little captain of your soul!... No!....Walter's got you to a 'T' and that's what bugs you. You were bloody awful to me you bastard! You took advantage of me when I was at my most vulnerable..... and I even had to help you do that! A bastard with a crutch, that's you!"

"Oh Brenda really, you are a card! Nobody's going to believe your contradictions!"

"Let the readers make up their own minds about you

John Julian-Walter's got the lowdown on you and you don't like it! You're squealing like a stuck pig. That's why you are here butting into Walter's story, trying to distract the readers' attention from the <u>real</u> you!"

"Oh and what are you doing here then? What are you so frightened of?"

"Frightened? Oh no! Walter knows a little bit about.... aspects of me. But at least I have the good grace to accept his insights and learn from them.

You're the frightened one John Julian –as usual, 'kicking against the pricks'"

"An unfortunate choice of metaphor Brenda, since that's precisely what you've been doing literally over the past twenty years!"

"You're a teacher John Julian. Try learning a little from Walter's story and stop turning it into low farce. I'm going!"

"All right! All right!...Goodbye!... She's right there, I'm giving myself some bad dialogue at the moment and I can't blame Walter for <u>that</u>!.......It was in the autumn term that Allison arrived on the scene...fresh, young, bubbly, intelligent... a real tonic to a moribund staff like ours...Now Walter has got all that quite wrong. He makes her out to be some kind of innocent with little personality, a bit like himself really.....Oh no! Allison was the life and soul of the place, at least to me!...Mind you, I nearly fluffed it...I had a chance..I...well....See for yourself!"

THE WENDY HOUSE

The Wendy House in Allison's classroom <u>was</u> rather splendid. Finely timbered and brightly painted with with winky-eyed windows and colourful curtains to match. It opened out grandly at the front to accommodate at least four infant-sized children or two medium-sized adults. It was positioned, in pride of place, right in the middle of the reception classroom. On the righthand side was a teacher's desk with a blackboard behind it. On the lefthand side were cupboards and a children's art display.

It is round about five thirty in the afternoon, mid October. Allison is crouching in the half-open 'Wendy House' trying to mend a light switch in the semi-darkness. The light flickers and there is a flash, an explosion and smoke.

Allison screams, "Oh my God!"

John Julian enters, in hat and coat carrying a briefcase. He puts on the classroom light.

"I must warn you that anything you say will taken down and may be used in evidence against you"

"Oh Mr Childs! You startled me!....I asked Walter Sidebrother to put a couple of sockets in my 'Wendy House' for me and I think he must have crossed a few wires somewhere!"

"Walter has many virtues but he's <u>not</u> a practical man. He's the very last person you should ask to do a thing like that for you..I beg your pardon, the last but one person..<u>I'm</u> the very last person you should ask to do something like that for you!"

She gets up and looks at him challengingly with those incredible blue eyes of hers: "Oh Mr Childs, I thought you were going to be useful!!"

Not aware of the emotional danger he is in and not caring overmuch, he puts his briefcase down and leans on the 'Wendy House' door close to Allison. He intimates to her the reasons for his ignorance.

"No. A long time ago when my father used to be

explaining the mysteries of electric circuits to my younger brother, I used to be practising the piano, so I missed out a very early stage."

"That's a fine excuse. It's only blessed socket after all (she sighs delightfully)..I suppose I'd better leave it to our resident handyman, Mr Dredge!"

"Oh no I wouldn't do that. But still, you're much too young to know what caretakers are like. They can't be trusted to put out the rubbish unless the regulation rubber gloves are provided and when there's a fuse that needs changing, they're phoning the borough engineers (mimicking Bob Dredge) 'Can't touch it Mr Childs sir! I'd have the H & S down on me like a ton of bricks. That's a job for the electricians sir!'" He engenders a giggle from her.

"Oh well I suppose I'd better leave it and get on with some painting."

She reaches for her overalls and gets a brush and paint, giving John Julian just enough time to think of what to do next.

"Now that's something I <u>can</u> help you with. As you know, Art is one of my responsibilities in this hall of learning of ours and I don't suppose there would be any objections from the Union of Wendy House Painters. What do you think?" He takes off his coat.

"No. O.K...There's an overall behind you on the chair.. But are you sure that you can spare the time Mr Childs? Haven't you got a family to go home to?"

"Allison, how long have you been at this school?"

"You know! Only a few weeks – Why?"

"Then it's high time that you knew that I'm a seedy old bachelor who is only too grateful for something to do after school to postpone the awful moment when he has to return to an empty flat –there should be someone playing 'Hearts and Flowers' at this point (he takes the paint and brush from Allison) By the way Allison, call me John Julian and <u>not</u> Mr Childs! It makes me feel less like a Deputy Head and more like a human being. Don't ever call me 'J.J'! I'm not in business. There <u>are</u> worse things than being a teacher!"

"Ok..John Julian... We'll start on the side pieces..We've got about half an hour before Mr Dredge kicks us out."

They paint on silently for a few minutes, giving John Julian ample time to calm his surprisingly juvenile emotions and muster his tactics. Allison breaks the silence.

"A penny for your thoughts Mr Childs –Sorry I mean John Julian!"

"I haven't got any Allison. There isn't a single coherent thought in my head at this time of the day. Teaching drains you of thought aswell as life or are you too young to notice yet?"

"I do feel a bit shattered from time to time but I do pick up a bit after dinner. Do stop going on about how old you are and how young I am. You ought to find some special hobbies to occupy yourself with in the evenings!"

At this point he thought he'd blown it, so he relaxed and didn't care.

"Strange as it may seem Allison <u>that</u> has been tried and found wanting. I used to go to evening classes at the Barnside Institute but I got tired and fed up with the new breed of lecturer that they have there now. They're usually bearded, disgustingly young and virile –they should be playing tennis or something not lecturing –open-necked silk shirts, and they sit <u>among</u> their students asking them for <u>their</u> opinions –seldom vouchsafing their own! I don't pay good money to be asked for <u>my</u> opinions on things. I go to learn about <u>theirs</u>, if they have any worth listening to!"

He had surprised himself with the vehemence of opinion

that his latent passion had brought on. But Allison soon put a damper on it.

"Oh but that's a bit old-fashioned coming from a teacher. Surely the modern way is to involve the student more and get him to work things out for himself through constant questioning and discussion –besides, <u>you've</u> got a beard!"

Knowing that he'd blown it, he started to get angry with himself and her. "That's not modern! It's an educational fallacy dating back to the ancient Greeks, as you ought to know –fresh from college!

It's based on the Socratic notion that truth arrives through discussion. It doesn't! –Only more discussion arrives through discussion, with the end result of proving that one person is cleverer or wiser than another. Hence grinning Socrates! It's all so egotistical! To be blunt –All it is, is intellectual wanking! With nothing coming out of it at the end except boredom, humiliation and exhaustion. Give me a good book any day!"

"So aren't you pulling the rug from under your own feet. Surely your teaching here must involve discussion with the children?"

"Not in my lessons Allison. I know a lot more than the children, that's not mere vanity, it's a fact. That's why I'm a teacher. They're there to listen to me and learn. Of course, things have to be explained, questions asked, misunderstandings dealt with. But this isn't asking the children for their opinions. It is helping them to form their own opinions and this is a very important distinction. Am I boring you?"

"Yes, but go on!!"

"It's an insult to a child's intelligence for him to be asked his opinion on things when his sole purpose for being in school is to be given the learning on which he may <u>later</u> be able to form opinions. It puts the children in a false position! No wonder there is so much indiscipline, rudeness and general bad manners in school nowadays. <u>We</u> encourage it!! (he points his paint brush at Allison in aggressive emphasis) <u>We</u> make them think they are adults before their time!!"

"You're not threatening me with that are you?"

"Sorry –I know I've lost the argument, so I resort to physical violence to get my way. I get carried away. Don't take me seriously, it's a little hobby horse of mine that I like to trot out on unsuspecting new-comers to the staff like you. It doesn't work anymore on Betty Teasdale, Perdita, Radcliffe, Hilary or even on Walter Sidebrother!"

"I didn't know you felt so strongly about things –I always thought of you as the staffroom cynic!"

His hopes were reviving!

"That's it! That's just it Allison. I <u>am</u> a cynic. I don't care one iota for most adult opinions and even less for all children's opinions. Nothing against adults. Nothing against children. I can't abide bullshit! And there's too much of it in education these days, particularly primary education."

"My, my, my! A deputy head teacher using words like 'wanking' and 'bullshit'" Her face reddened. He was now the naughty boy to be punished.

"Tut tut! Undignified is it? You <u>are</u> old fashioned Miss Prestatyn! Aren't the elderly allowed to use expressive words like that or is it just the privilege of the young?"

"No. Just the self-indulgence of the immature of all ages, actually."

"Touche. I was about to ask you to drop all this and come and join me for a drink to send us both on our way home. But am I pushing my luck?"

He was indeed but he had reached that pitch of desperation that he was prepared to gamble all.

"No!" She put her paint pot down and started taking off her overalls, "I'll buy you a drink at the Bear's Hotel. It's far enough away from here for people not to raise their eyebrows when a probationer buys a drink for the Deputy Head of Belle View Primary School –Unless it is beneath your dignity to accept?"

He was triumphant as he took off his overalls.

"If I still have any dignity at my age I deserve to be shot! Come on probationer!"

INTERLUDE 3
ALLISON BEGS TO DIFFER!

ALLISON IS LOOKING VERY DIFFERENT TO THE WAY SHE has been portrayed. She is wearing jeans, is smoking and looks a lot more confident than we might have thought. She holds forth with vigor!

"No, no, it won't do Walter. You see. Walter is totally confused about men and women. He doesn't know who he is sexually and so he is isn't able to read other people right either. What happened was a good deal more complicated than he makes out. Actually I was the one who proposed to John Julian that we should go for the drink. He told me all about himself in the pub-poured his pathetic little soul out he did. It was obvious that he had been besotted by Brenda and she had given him the runaround —and he had been quite badly shaken by the experience. He was like a little whipped pup when he came to me —all ragged and wild-eyed and I wasn't very sympathetic to be honest. But he needed a shoulder to cry on and I provided that shoulder, but only that shoulder!"

"Allison are we following the same story? It's obvious from that last truthful scene that you're all looks and no heart but with a little condescending pity thrown in. Walter missed out on only one thing —your obviously strong passions. But how was the lad to know? Even an old heterosexual campaigner like myself couldn't stir those flames after months of stoking away at the grate!"

"Oh go to hell!!" She storms off, leaving John Julian to address the readers.

"....And what next? Some staffroom small talk –Oh what a relief from the turgid emotions and the savage breast to hear the conversational inconsequentialities of Mrs Teasdale & Co –Music to my ears! Walter you deserve a prize for this bit of the story.

"Ladies and gentlemen, before we move on to the

next part of Walter's sad little account of our lives, may I, Elizabeth Barratt Teasdale, take this opportunity of saying that the behaviour of certain 'characters' in this story have been disgraceful. Moreover it ill-behoves such 'characters' to try to move out of the story and try to justify themselves to the readers...Everyone has the right to an entertaining suspension of disbelief for the duration but in between times we need to be able to go to the loo or have a drink and a sandwich having put the story firmly out of our minds. These 'characters' are confusing the readers. Please <u>believe</u> me dear readers –<u>None</u> of it is true! It's just entertainment. Don't be fooled by the author's tricks."

John Julian returns and pops his head over her shoulder!

"So Betty! What are you doing here?"

"Isn't it obvious? I'm trying to prevent the readers from being hoodwinked by the likes of you!"

"Oh, I see, so they can be more easily hoodwinked by the likes of you!"

"I'm not rising to your bait John Julian and I hope the readers don't either. I think I know these readers. They are a decent, level-headed lot and they'll discard this story with the contempt it deserves <u>after</u> they have extracted the minuscule amount of entertainment it contains."

It is the author's prerogative to intervene when things get out of hand in his narrative and this situation is no exception.

"Excuse me! Do you mind? I'm trying to get on with this story which you are both attempting to sabotage at this moment. Please leave the readers alone. Let them make their own minds up. We have so many things in store for them!"

Mrs Teasdale has to have the last word.

"Do forgive us!"

They all exit together. John Julian shrugging his shoulders and splaying his hands in mock despair.

Staffroom Games!

Let's get on, as Howard Bulcastle would say. We are some weeks into the term now. Let's take a peep into the staffroom as the breaktime bell goes. John Julian sits at the staffroom table, head down, marking books. Avis Gunn is looking for something again and spends the best part of her breaktime vainly searching the staffroom. Brunhilde Waizmann is making the tea in a large teapot with all the precise dignity of a chef preparing for a royal banquet –Oh lucky Belle View!

Avis shrills, "I'm positive I left it somewhere in here!"

John Julian, without looking up "Avis! How on earth can you lose an overhead projector?"

Avis screetches like a demented owl, "Really Mr Childs!! I said an overhead projector <u>transparency</u>! As I say to my children, if only we all <u>listened</u> a little more there would be fewer misunderstandings and the world would be a happier place!"

John Julian aims and fires, "I'm always listening to you Avis but you never tell me anything I want to hear!"

Brunhilde endeavours to help, "What actually was on the transparency Miss Gunn??"

"Nicholas Woods thingee –You know, animated instruments of the orchestra in coloured transpaseal. It took me two days and two nights to do it and I planned to start my lessons today. Bother, bother, bother, bother!!"

"Oh come and have a cup of tea my love. I expect it will turn up like your talking cuckoo clock!"

"Mrs Waizmann!! Transparencies don't talk but they evidently walk! I do remember seeing it in your office but I forgot to pick it up because I was on the phone about Mr Higgins' talk on reading!"

"No my dear! You didn't leave it in <u>my</u> office!" Brunhilde perches on the best Parker Knoll seat, normally reserved for Mrs Teasdale, and drinks her coffee in a pose that is both studied and disinterested at the same time,

"I expect Howard Bulcastle has got it in his office somewhere. He's got everything else that's missing from the school in there, so I wouldn't be at all surprised if he'd got your animated animals!"

Feathers fly, "They're not 'animated animals Mrs Waizmann! They're animated instruments of the orchestra (John Julian joins in in unison) in coloured transpaseal!!!"

At this point Brenda and Walter duet acrimoniously as they enter the staffroom. Walter begins the refrain:

"There was no need for you to sh-shout like that at those boys Brenda! It really upset them. We had a cup match after school and we didn't have complete sets. They were only l-looking!"

Brenda had had a bad morning and Walter was going to pay for it:

"So tell your bloody chess team Walter to keep out of my needlework cupboard or they'll be losing more than chess pieces!"

"But there was no need to shout! That's six pieces lost in three days –three black pawns, one bishop –white bishop and two white pawns!"

Avis fluttering nearby, "Mr Dredge said he'd picked up a 'white queen' in the boys toilets the other day. This shelf's in a state no wonder things get lost!"

John Julian picking up the pieces, "Ooh did he? White queen eh!!"

Brenda gets one in quick, "Not your sort of white queen duckie! Anyway I thought you only played the black pieces these days" (winking broadly and cackling).

Avis, with bird-like alacrity, spots Walter 'illegally'

taking coffee from a jar and pecks him mercilessly (though it won't bring back her transparencies):

"Walter Sidebrother! You leave that coffee jar alone until you've paid your dues and joined our 'Coffee Club!'"

"I have joined your precious 'Coffee Club' –Just now!"

"Not until you've paid your dues!!"

John Julian protects, "Leave the lad alone Avis! I thought you were looking for something?"

This is cue for Brenda to rise unsmiling and go to the window where she lights a cigarette and stares out:

"We're all looking for something and not finding it, that's the trouble!" She cackles menacingly.

Hilary, Radcliffe and Perdita bustle in.

Hilary blusters "Did my Desmond call this morning Mrs Waizmann?"

Brunhilde, hackles visibly rising, "I beg your pardon!"

"Did my husband call? He said he's let me know if my car got through its M.O.T.!!"

"See here young Hilary Trumble! Some people seem to think that I have nothing better to do than take personal phone messages all day. You know Mr Bulcastle rule. No personal phone calls before twelve thirty."

"Look! He can't phone in the afternoons! He's out taking Driving Tests.

Surely it can't be too much trouble to make a wee exception to the rule once in a while. After all, you are the school secretary and not the Lady Mayoress of Barnfield!!"

"Thank you very much!" She drops her coffee cup on the floor and storms out.

Walter notices, "You've upset Brunhilde now!!"

Brenda concludes, "Bang goes our sports fixture lists for this term. We won't get them typed now! Not if we go down on our bended knees! Did you have to be so characteristically rude Hilary?"

"'Fraid so Brenda! I can't take any more of her pouting and pontificating!"

Mrs Teasdale enters with exquisite timing to lend her moral support to Brunhilde.

"<u>Now</u> who's upset Brunhilde?! She's gone to the ladies' crying her eyes out. It's not the first time this week either!" She sits in her special seat.

"Get me a cup of tea Walter, there's a love. Howard Bulcastle shouted at her because she's got Picasso prints up in his office and now this!"

John Julian patronises, "It's not just the prints though Betty. She sometimes behaves as though she's the headmistress and actually you know, she's rather an inefficient secretary!"

Mrs Teasdale rises to it, "Nonsense! Howard Bulcastle would be lost without her. After all, she is <u>his</u> secretary and not ours!"

Hilary parries, "That's just my point! She's the <u>school</u> secretary but she doesn't do anything for the rest of us unless we roll a red carpet out for her!"

Brenda, in a mellower mood, "There <u>is</u> something in what you say Hilary but Mrs Teasdale's right too. Brunhilde can speak and write very good English which Howard Bulkcastle must find very useful on occasions."

"Yes, she does have better taste than he does in most things. Anway, I prefer her Picasso prints to his 'Stag At Bay'!" mused John Julian.

Avis, despairingly, "Please! Has anyone seen my 'Nicholas Wood Animated Instruments of the Orchestra'... (the whole staff in unison)..in coloured transpaseal!!"

Mrs Teasdale, resuming her knitting, "Miss Gunn

would you please get down off the top of that cupboard, you're making me nervous!"

Radcliffe sympathises, "Perhaps if we all had a search round, we could find this transparency for Avis!"

Brenda, unsympathises, "She's been searching for that blessed thing since the beginning of the week. I don't believe it exists. I think she's looking for something else. She and I have both been looking for something all our lives —right Avis?"

"I don't know what you're talking about Brenda Gratten. I think you're just being facetious."

"Well, if either of you <u>do</u> find something perhaps you'd be good enough to tell me. I'm off to see if Bottomly is doing his playground duty. If anyone needs me, don't tell them where I am will you!" John Julian wittily exits, just as Howard Bulcastle enters and bellows across the staffroom:

"Miss O'Toole, could I have a word? That nurse woman who examines their hair is here. Could you see to her?" Perdita exits with Howard.

Brenda mimics mercilessly, "'That nurse woman who examines their hair' -Good grief! Come back Brunhilde Waizmann all is forgiven!!"

Hilary still aggrieved, "Desmond is pretty fed up with that woman's rudeness I'll tell you. She can be so intimidating over the phone. She makes Belle View School seem like Buckingham Palace."

"That's <u>why</u> she's so useful to Howard!" Mrs Teasdale added.

"Still! Desmond does give as much as he takes so I expect Brunhilde can't be too happy about passing on his messages"

Walter gets excited, "Y-Your D-Desmond seems to be

quite a lad..I must admit Hilary, I for one had gotten a bit fed up hearing 'Desmond this' and 'Desmond that'....

"Cheek!!"

"....But ever since you told that story about how he was arrested for sh-shouting abuse at the police outside your actual police station...I w-warmed to him..Oh G-God! M-My stammer is coming b-b-back. Someone b-b-bang me on the b-b-back. It's the only cure!!"

Brenda smiles in obligation. She jumps up and hits him so hard that he falls off his chair.

"Oh Jesus! Not that hard you s-s-silly s-s-s-soft fat-head!!"

"My pleasure Walter! Now I must tidy that needlework cupboard!"

Radcliffe mother-earths him, "You all right Walter? That was a nasty thump!!

You _are_ a fool tempting Brenda like that!"

Allison creeps in looking a little dishevelled and spotted with paint.

Mrs Teasdale commiserates, "Where've you been? Sit down Allison, you look all in!" She puts a cushion on a chair next to hers.

"It's only morning break and I feel I've been in that classroom all day.

Pinky Pemberton pulled a whole tray of paint jars on top of me. Alice Waters said I looked like a rainbow. That's what they call creativity I suppose."

"Never mind love. I think you've got most of it off. I feel perpetually tired Allison. I think it's the occupational disease of teachers. You always hear about the miners don't you, and how they have to retire early with silicosis and that sort of thing. But nobody wants to hear about nervous breakdowns that teachers succumb to. It's all in the mind you see. A dirty, black-faced miner with a wheezing chest and a Welsh accent tugs at the heart strings. But a clean, middle-class teacher with a twitching face, a stammer and an Oxford accent gets no sympathy at all —rather, derisive laughter!" Mrs Teasdale finishes with a smug lick of her lips.

Walter self-consciously pitches in, "And they get no compensation either! Still I'd sooner be a teacher than a m-m-miner any day!"

Hilary rejoinders, "You'll get no sympathy from me Walter Sidebrother! Besides you don't have an Oxford accent!"

Bob Dredge enters —Behind him comes John Julian. Bob holds up to the horror-stricken gaze of all – A black bit of lace frillies!

"May I have your attention please! One of my cleaning ladies found a pair of split-crotch lace underwear in the 'Wendy House' in the Old Hall.. I don't know whether.."

John Julian interrupts, retrieves the item in question and ushers him unceremoniously out!

"Thank you Mr Dredge! I'll see to it!"

Allison is justifiably needled, "He knows perfectly well that that's my 'Wendy House'! He's supposed to be repairing it!! As a matter of fact I was given the material in question by Guy Penchard's mother to make glove puppets!..... Well, don't all look at me like that!! One of the children must have dropped them in there!"

Hilary, knowingly, "I expect they did!"

Walter explores the comic possibilities to relieve the tension.

"I w-wonder what else he f-f-found there! My kids are making spaceships!"

Mrs Teasdale, outrage simmering, "Don't let your mind dwell on it Walter! It'll only bring on your stammer and you won't be able to take my children for 'Read Me a Story' after play. Rumplestiltskin is not the easiest of words to say at the best of times. I hope you haven't forgotten that you're reading a story to us after play??"

"N-N-No Mrs Teasdale. I always look forward to it."

John Julian passes the panties to Allison, "I wished I looked forward to something. Here Allison take these before I start making glove puppets!"

The bell for the end of break goes. Everyone prepares to leave for their classes. John Julian ushers them out.

"Back to the grindstone! Come on folks!" cries Hilary boisterously.

"Oh Hilary, before you go, send me Yuka Saikarmo, I want her to translate for me. Hiriuchi in Mr Jenson's class is crying because he says Carol Barnes has got his trolls – if you please! I don't want to know what he's jabbering about but we'd better sort it out..I don't want hari kari at Belle View during my Deputy Head stewardship!"

"O.k. and don't forget you're taking my lot for 'Singing Together' at eleven thirty five!"

"I thought you were seeing Mrs Drummond from the P.T.A. at eleven thirty John Julian?" reminded Radcliffe.

"Oh God no! That's all I need. It'll be another one of her 'Knit A Dwarf for Christmas' schemes, I'm sure of it! Radcliffe, deal with her will you? I'll give you a free period next week!!"

"Done!!"

Mrs Teasdale's simmering outrage finally boils over.

"Mr Childs that was uncalled for! Mrs Drummond has given her all to this school! She's worked like a black for the P.T.A. and much thanks she gets for it!"

'Thou hast delivered her into mine hands Oh Lord,' thinks John Julian.

"An unfortunate choice of metaphor Betty, considering that a third of our children are West Indian. Personally, I think we would all be able to breathe a little more easily if she gave a little <u>less</u> of herself!"

Mrs Teasdale starts to move out and reaches the door as Walter appeases.

"I-I'll be down in f-five minutes Mrs Teasdale!"

"You'll be down <u>now</u> Walter! The bell went five minutes ago! What is happening to this school!" She gives John Julian a withering look and slams the door behind her.

"Don't worry about it Walter. Just as long as you can pronounce Rumplestiltskin correctly, you'll soon be back in her good books –and much good it may do you!"

"It's not Rumplestiltskin I'm worried about Mr Childs. It's the wicked fairy!"

John Julian bottoms him out of the door, "Oh go on with you!"

INTERLUDE 4

A Time for Prayer!

" JOHN JULIAN <u>AGAIN</u>...SETTLING INTO THE STORY ARE you? Good. Is Mrs Teasdale beginning to get on your nerves?...... I thought so, good........It was about this time that I started thinking about how I could solve the problem of Betty Teasdale. At first I thought straight suicide on my part would nicely solve a hell of a lot of problems all at once. But the thought of sweet Allison gave me some slight hope for myself. So I thought, why not take it to the Lord, pray about it! Coming from a dyed-in-the-wool old atheist like me it was a desperate measure. But desperate times require desperate remedies, as the cliché goes. I prayed hard.............Dear Lord! Take Thy servant Elizabeth Barratt Teasdale to Thyself. She has served Thee well and deserves her reward...............No such luck....After a month's praying and some discreet sticking of pins in old school photographs, she was still as hale and hearty as ever and giving Walter as much stick as ever she did..(he lights a cigarette)...... Old Walter's quite merciless on himself isn't he? No such masochistic tendencies in me I can assure you...Don't think I'm enjoying talking to you like this, it just helps pass the time, Lord knows I have enough of it on my hands these days....Still, there is the memory of sweet Allison..ignore her protestations dear readers...Here's a nice little scene..Well done Walter, full marks for this one!"

WENDY HOUSE GAMES

My, how time flies when you're having fun in the classroom but it flies even faster when you're having fun out of the classroom too. The evenings are drawing in and we're into November now. It's after school –about five thirty and Bob Dredge is anxiously looking at his watch and ready to stop any extracurricular fun if he can. There is a little glow of light in a little house in a certain reception classroom. John Julian and Allison are still painting that 'Wendy House' –they've got round to the red roof!

John Julian breaks the silence, "It doesn't really need a gloss finish you know. It's a waste of P.T.A. money Allison –Mrs Drummond would have a blue fit if she knew what you were spending your class allocation on!"

He laughs at his own mimicry of Mrs Drummond's fiscal small-mindedness.

Allison responds in kind, "Mrs Drummond may be able to dictate to Mr Bulcastle but she can't tell me what to spend in my own classroom. Besides I did say that I wanted it for art materials."

"It's funny how Bulcastle cowers in front of Mrs Drummond and minions from the education offices –Yet he walks all over the rest of us. Pass the rag will you, I've dropped some paint on your 'alphabetical floorboards'!"

"Oh no John Julian! They were only painted on last week and varnished"

She comes round to examine, "I put some paper there to stop messy Deputy Heads from spoiling my nice new floor. Just a moment! I can't see any mess!" he grabs her round the waist, "Got you!!" But she adroitly escapes to the other side of the 'Wendy House': "John Julian really! Somebody might come in! I'd never be able to show my face again if people thought......"

"....You were responding to the attentions of an older man?"

"Don't be ridiculous! Age has nothing whatever to do with it! Just get on with your painting! You're a very naughty Deputy Head Teacher!"

"...And you are a very wise old probationary teacher!"

"Less of the old if you don't mind. In case you'd forgotten, there is a considerable difference in our ages!"

"Yes, I had done some rough calculations along those lines myself. I'm beginning to think that you are too old for me Allison!"

"You ought to think of your career you know. One day you'll be a head!"

"I've no desire, no ambition to be a Head. I know they say that the Deputy Headship is the elephants' graveyard for senior teachers but it's as far as I'll ever get. I don't feel the need to lick any more boots –the polish is thick enough on my tongue as it is!"

"Don't you feel that you'd like to run your own school?"

"I don't think I could run a whelk stall to be honest with you. Anyway, I'm not interested in running anything –just so long as I can enjoy the camaraderie of the staffroom, playing the piano, painting pictures, writing a little –I don't want anything else. All Heads are interested in is power, a spurious influence over others. They're nearly all the same, insensitive, egocentric and deeply and single-mindedly interested in schools. That last quality is their most serious defect, in my view. It shows a lack of imagination."

"Aren't Heads supposed to be interested in their schools?"

"I don't like people who take things too seriously!"

"That explains a lot!"

He walks round to her but she doesn't escape this time. He points his brush at a gable end: "You've missed a bit... there!"

"Oh go on with you!"

They paint for a minute or two in silence. Allison breaks the ice.

"Do you mind if I ask you a personal question??"

John Julian anticipates, "'Why did you never marry, John Julian Childs?'"

"Yes!!"

"....because I don't like people who take things too seriously, I guess. Come on let's leave this, the pubs must be open by now. It's my turn to buy if I remember rightly."

"Well let's finish this little bit, it won't take too long –We're nearly at the eaves."

Mrs Teasdale appears at the open door, surveying the scene and drawing her predigested conclusions.

"Sorry to trouble you Mr Childs –I was wondering if you could give me a lift to the bus stop when you've finished. Brian telephoned from the office to tell me his car won't start so he can't pick me up. It's such a nuisance and I've got to see Mrs Bronwick at the Infirmary at eight she's got c-a-n-c-e-r!"

"Certainly Betty. I can do better than that –I'm going over Hampstead way so I Can give you lift to the door."

"That's decent of you. You're late tonight Allison. Won't Stanley be worried about you?"

"Oh Stanley and I split up last month Mrs Teasdale!"

"Oh I <u>am</u> sorry Allison.......I think it's such a shame when young marriages break up like that.....You really must be going through the mill!!"

"Oh nothing like that. We weren't exactly married or anything. We'd been living together for about eighteen months and –it just didn't work out!"

"Oh I see! Well I suppose it doesn't matter then. I'll just go and get my things together John Julian and I'll meet you by your car. How long do you intend to be?" Allison turns her head away in obvious annoyance.

"About ten or fifteen minutes at the most."

Allison defiantly, "We've nearly finished Mrs Teasdale. What do you think?"

"I don't really know quite what to think!" She looks suspiciously at the two of them and then down at the 'Wendy House'... "I don't know why you want to use a full-gloss finish on a 'Wendy House' –but still..."

Allison provocatively, "We won't be long –We'll be out in five minutes, I reckon –See you at the car!"

"You're coming aswell are you? I thought you lived over Harrow way?"

"No, I've got a flat near Camden Town now!"

"Oh!"

John Julian guiltily, "I'm buying her a drink on the way home Betty –I hope you don't mind. She was kind enough to let me help her with the 'Wendy House'. So I thought, one good turn deserves another. What say you?"

"Why should I mind? Can't say I approve of drink because I know what can happen afterwards. But still, as long as you deliver _me_ safely home – stone cold sober John Julian, _I_ won't complain.... I'll be off then –see you in a minute." She waddles off, walking stick cluck clucking disapprovingly.

Allison let's fly, "Did you hear what that woman was implying? Does _her_ husband drink??"

"What, old Ernest? Good grief no. If he did she'd soon find out what can happen afterwards and then maybe she wouldn't be so hard on the rest of us! Come on, let's finish and go!"

"You can drop me off first if you like, I don't feel like a drink now!"

"Oh don't be ridiculous. You mustn't let that old witch get to you so easily. She's a merchant of guilt and thoroughly enjoys disconcerting people. The best way to deal with her type is take no notice of her!"

Allison resignedly, "I suppose you're right!"

They take off their overalls.

"Allison, I never know whether I'm right or not. But if there is a flash of lightning and a roll of thunder and the car crashes into a tree —then we're all wrong and it doesn't matter anyway. Come on!"

INTERLUDE 5

Be Nice to Turn this into a Play!

WALTER WAS TEMPTED TO PUT IN A FLASH OF lightning and a roll of thunder at this point but decided that such providential timing would not be felicitous. But it did make him wonder whether to turn his story into a play. John Julian had already entertained the idea but had forgotten all about it as he was enjoying himself now:

"I liked that. Walter doesn't know the half of it. But the half he knows, he knows quite well! All thoughts of murder <u>almost</u> went out of my head after that little episode, seeing Betty on the rack of her self-righteousness gave me some wickedly good vibrations!"

A whole lot of them now vie for the readers' sympathetic attention and Walter tries to quieten his prose down:

"Oh stop it all of you! John Julian you're attempting to hijack the whole story. You're not the only one in it you know!"

Brenda vies, "I think this sort of melodramatic interruption is ridiculous. You'll drive the readers away in droves and I hope you're satisfied John Julian!"

"..A great deal more satisfied than you'll <u>ever</u> be Brenda!"

Mrs Teasdale expatiates, "Listen to him! Walter can't you write him out of this story? Is it too late?? And frankly, I'd like a little more positive portrayal of myself if you don't mind. You're making me out to be some kind of monster, it really isn't fair. The readers deserve better."

Walter placates, "You're fine in the next scene Mrs Teasdale!"

"I sincerely hope so Walter Sidebrother!"

John Julian is appalled and offended, "I'm not standing here to listen to this!" He stalks off.

"Neither are we!!" They all stalk off.

Morning Assembly

It is some days later. It is that great showpiece of Bell View school life –the weekly full school assembly. It is set in the large hall which also doubles as a gymnasium. The staff are arrayed in a line in front with Howard Bulcastle and John Julian Childs on a raised dais in the middle. Behind them an overhead projector screen will display the hymn 'All Things Bright And Beautiful' in which the readers will be asked to join in. Also some transpaseal pictures will be shown to illustrate Howard Bulcastle's theme for the assembly. The children troop in to the loud sounds of a suitably impressive, virtuosic piece played on the piano by Hilary Trumble. As she goes in to the second movement she is mercifully stopped by Howard Bulcastle.

"Thank you Mrs Trumble! How fortunate we are children to have such a talented staff at our school. Let us bow our heads in prayer and thank God for the talents that he has bestowed on...."

He is interrupted by John Julian whispering loudly, "Mr Bottomly's class appear not to have arrived Mr Bulcastle –should we start without them?"

Howard, visibly annoyed, shouts, "Dunkley! Go and see what's keeping Mr Bottomly's class please!"

He motions to Mrs Trumble who continues her virtuosic piece to the obvious fidgeting boredom of the children and the resigned acquiescence of the staff.

Eventually Bulcastle denotes by a movement of his head that the class has arrived and motions Mrs Trumble to stop.

"Once again thank you Mrs Trumble. Let us bow our heads in prayer and thank God for the talents that he bestowed in his mercy on our school. Mrs Trumble's talents at the piano... Mr Childs' talents in the fields of

Music and Art... Mrs Ball's talents in the artistic field aswell (he coughs)... Mrs Teasdale's talents in Handicraft, Pottery, Needlework and Bible Study... Mr Sidebrother's gifts in Drama, Metalwork and Chess... Mrs Prestatyn has contributed in a very inspired way in her Leaf Collecting Club not forgetting Miss Gunn's excellent work in Creative Maths and in her 'Lively Library' Circle... Mr Bottomly too has transformed our football team and with the help of God's spirit has brought them to the threshold of a bronze medal in Division Three of the Barnside Junior League (staff wince)... Let us also thank the Lord for Mrs Gratten's work in P.E. and Netball and....erhm.

(Brenda whispers to him in disgust}..that's right, Needlework too... Finally last but not least, Mrs O'Toole has given so much of herself in charity work but kept a bit behind for her Gardening Club (staff wince again). Thank you Lord. Amen....Now Mrs Trumble perhaps you could give us 'All Things Bright And Beautiful' –Not the full concert version you understand..Thank you Mrs Trumble..

"Hilary glowing, "Thank you Mr Bulcastle!" She launches on a much-embellished introduction to it.

"Mrs Trumble!!??"

"Sorry Mr Bulcastle, I got carried away again!"

John Julian mumbles, "..and so she ought to be!"

They all sing the first chorus of the hymn –Bulcastle motioning to the children to sing up. Walter nervously operates the overhead projector, getting a map of the world on the screen before he finally arrives at the second verse. Mrs Teasdale sings this solo, her breast heaving and her voice trembling like a big-bosomed thrush. Afterwards Bulcastle stops the proceedings because he has detected 'sniggering'.

"Stokeley McHughes! Get out of this hall now and stand

outside my office and take that 'action man' with you! The very idea!"

Howard once again motions to the children to carry on with the next chorus which is followed by the last verse sung solo by a tremulous Avis Gunn.

Then comes the final chorus. Each member of staff can be seen joining in except John Julian who looks totally disinterested and Walter Sidebrother who looks totally nerve-racked as the O.H.P. blows up, with much smoke, at the end of the hymn. Walter collapses and is taken out by Radcliffe and Perdita. John Julian eventually takes over the O.H.P. which appears to work again after much persuasion by Howard Bulcastle.

Howard resumes, "Well I think that's back in business again (he motions to the staff and children to sit down) Children as you can see from the picture on the screen.... erhm thank you Mr Childs....God is <u>very</u> big! (pointing to a picture of a large man with a beard) and we are <u>very</u> small (pointing to a picture of much smaller man with a bald head and spectacles)...Now if God gets disappointed in us, he will show his disappointment in no uncertain way! (shows another picture of that same large man putting his foot in the face of the same much smaller man, broken glasses lying nearby)...God likes us most of the time but sometimes when we don't do as we're told, he gets upset, as you can see in the picture...God who is very much bigger thas us is showing us just how upset he can be because a certain somebody <u>didn't</u> look after his gerbil! (points to a small brown blob at the feet of the much smaller man)...You may all be wondering who that little boy is and what he actually did with his gerbil!.... (he looks around seeking out the guilty).....Well, I'd certainly like to know who he was! But we did find his gerbil thanks to Percy Horsfall's sharp little eyes and Mr Dredge's expert little hands....It was found <u>under</u> the library carpet!! <u>Not</u> a very pleasant place to find any living creature! Especially with the Countries of the World Bookcase resting on top of it!! I only hope that nasty little boy or girl...but I think it was a boy....is SATISFIED (very loud and almost hysterical, saliva dripping) BECAUSE IF I FIND OUT WHO IT IS, I DON'T KNOW WHAT I SHALL DO!! (wipes the foam from his mouth)...Let us pray. Hands joined! Eyes closed!...Oh Lord, in Thy infinite wisdom, power and love, lead us by the hand to whomsoever it was that did this unspeakably foul deed that we may bring Thy justice to bear upon him that he may be sorry for his illdoing and that he may never do it again whilst he dwell on the premises of Belle View School. Amen... Notices, Mrs Gratten's crochet group will be meeting as usual at 1.00p.m., in Mrs Gratten's room, every day except Thursday..."

Brenda outbursting, "Friday!!"

"Sorry Mrs erhm Gratten. Friday. Crochet group meeting every day except Friday, in Mrs Gratten's room at 1.00p.m.... Mr Sidebrother's chess club will be meeting as usual on Thursday after school in the library...Miss Prestatyn's thriving 'Leaf Collecting Circle' will also be meeting on Thursday after school in her room...I'm afraid you won't be able to collect leaves <u>and</u> play chess, you'll just have to make a choice.... Will Dinner Monitors and Tidy Officers please report to Mr Childs' immediately after this assembly.

Now I come to a somewhat delicate matter –Toilets! These brand new toilets have been provided for your benefit, not for mine. It doesn't matter to me or to your teachers that you have toilets to go to. They are for you. But you must treat them properly. They are not for playing in or for going to every five minutes when you should be learning things in your classrooms that your parents have paid for through the rates or through their noses in some cases (staff wince or cover themselves in embarrassment)...Now if Mr Dredge complains to me again of things stuffed down the toilets –action men, chess pieces, plasticine, Maths exercise paper, pencils and Uncle Tom Cobbley and all, I shall have no alternative...Get out Johnson!..I shall have no alternative but to close these beautiful new toilets and you'll just have to make do with the old outside ones..Mr Childs has appointed six toilet monitors from the top junior classes to be on duty during the two breaks and lunchtime, and they will make sure that our wonderful, clean new toilets, that we were so lucky to get so promptly from the council, are not abused by the feckless and the uncaring...Lydia Greaves and Parmadiaz Framsian of 4Q, Maurice Johns and Arita Singh of 4L, Mercy Gripps and Kingsley Carmichael of 4Z, see Mr Childs immediately after this assembly.

Finally, let me end on a cheerful note –Mrs Teasdale is leaving us at Christmas (staff wince again, Mr Childs smiles!)...after thirty eight years of devoted service to the Borough of Barnside and Belle View School in particular... She wishes to mark her retirement in a very special way this term, by launching her 'Send Jesus to Africa' appeal –which I hope you'll support in various ways and in particular of course we need generous donations of cash to help send those missionaries to Africa to spread the word of God... Mrs Teasdale herself will give an assembly tomorrow to tell us all precisely what she intends...Perhaps you could lead us into the final prayers Mrs Teasdale??"

"Thank you Mr Bulcastle. I'd be glad to. (Looking at Bulcastle) By all means let us be cheerful about departures! I'm a great one for being cheerful in the Lord –but I don't know just how cheerful I'm going to be by Christmas time!.... (addressing the children)..However, if that naughty little boy who took my gerbil would come and apologise sometime, I think I might be just a widget more cheerful by Christmas!

Boys and girls –You don't know how lucky you are. If you ever get hungry for the word of God, all you've got to do is pop down Belle View Lane and you've got at least six different churches to choose from, an embarrass du richesse as the French would day, an embarrassment of riches. But if you were a little boy or girl living in Africa, you might have to walk miles and miles and miles to get spiritual sustenance. That's not very nice is it? (staff wince, eyes heavenward).. So let us remember in our prayers all those boys and girls who need a more convenient place to hear the word of God... Hands together! ..Eyes closed!..Dear Lord. Turn the hearts of Thy people that they mayest give of themselves in a generous spirit, that the Reverend Fetchley Arthur Warmpit's Fund for Christian Missions may grow and grow daily, ever increasing and piling higher to Thy greater glory....Let us pray that these generous gifts may help to build places of worship within a stone's throw of where Thy African people dwelleth so that they may be able to worship more conveniently for Thy name's sake. Amen." Everyone joins in -'Amen'.

Bulcastle rises and tilts his uncombed head deferentially towards his most senior teacher, "Thank you Mrs Teasdale!"

His demeanour then changes as he looks out at the serried ranks of the children!

.Right!...Arms folded! Eyes to the front!..Mrs Trumble if you would like to play the lead-off music, we'll all return to our classrooms..Starting with the fourth years....get out Jones and stand by more door!"

Hilary, with head rocking and arms pounding, thunders out a loud virtuosic March. The children file out and the staff drift off the platform to their respective classes. Howard Bulcastle is left alone in the hall and....

INTERLUDE 6
BULCASTLE JUSTIFIES!

"LADIES AND GENTLEMEN, AS HEAD TEACHER OF Belle View Primary School, and on behalf of the staff, I'd just like to say a few words of appreciation for you the logsuffering readers..You've been great –considering there hasn't been much to be great about. The author of this story, Walter Sidebrother, is on a Scale A Post here at this school and as far as I am concerned he'll be staying on a Scale A until the end of his career.. Certain scandalous allegations have been made concerning my association with Mrs Gratten! Can I say here and now that I don't consider a few fumbles and kisses in the stock cupboard anything like serious enough to be considered as a full-blown affair – whatever the rumour-mongers may say!!"

Brenda, in defiant mood, "Howard! Come on Howard! Just because you were a limp failure, there's no need to turn it into a boring little virtue!"

"I think my part is substantial enough Mrs Gratten, But it does seem to shrink whenever you are around, as you do so like to be the star of the show!"

"Never! It would appear that Mrs Teasdale is the star of the show! I don't know what she is belly-aching about! Every other scene seems to feature her, but then this oughtn't to surprise us as Walter, bless his little cotton socks, is only following his crystal-clear obsessions!"

John Julian, overacting grotesquesly, "There is only one star of this little show folks! (grimacing) Need I say more? Just have the patience to follow the story to its bitter end and you'll see!"

"Well Mr Childs, I think as my deputy you ought to feature a little less prominently in the plot than I do...But you do appear to be providing the connecting thread and in that sense you are the star and much good it may do you!"

"Howard   coming   from   you   that   is   a   true

acknowledgement! Never mind! There's a lovely little cameo of you coming up in the next scene and Brenda it's your big moment too!"

He winks complicitly at the reader.

MORE WENDY HOUSE GAMES!

Some days later we are in a darkened Nursery classroom with one light shining brightly in the 'Wendy House' which is folded back to reveal the corpulent frame of Howard Bulcastle on his knees inside with his big bag of tools at his side. He's putting the finishing touches to the electrics and Allison stands by admiringly (at first).

"Oh thank you Mr Bulcastle - I didn't think <u>anyone</u> could do it, I've tried everybody!"

"Well...I'm not just <u>anybody</u> Miss Prestatyn –I'm your headmaster..Now look (he leans forward and grabs some wires) It's just a simple matter of distinguishing between your blue and red wires and you (he gets up) as a mere woman should at least know your colours so..."

"That's a fairly unsubtle sexist remark if ever I heard one –I suppose you don't think women are capable of practical science is that it?"

"Women scientists and engineers? They have a few in Eastern Europe don't they –Hairy legs, short cropped hair, deep voices... You can keep them! (he starts to walk out)..I prefer real women like you Miss Prestatyn (he turns at the door)...and don't be ashamed of the fact...If you want me you know where to find me!"

Allison pauses, stunned, aghast and aggrieved, "Christ!!"

John Julian comes in from the opposite door.

"No not Christ! Sorry to disappoint you Allison —It's only the Deputy Messiah, that's all!"

"Bulcastle!!"

"Yes, I saw him trundle out just now. What an endearing man he is. Upset you has he?"

"He's got about as much tact and diplomacy as Genghis Khan! He's your original male chauvinist pig!"

John Julian inspects the work, "Well, he's mended your lights for you, aren't you grateful?"

"Grovellingly, obsequiously grateful of course! That's the only kind of gratitude he ever seems to earn from anybody!"

"Oh just be grateful and leave it at that. Coming for a drink?"

"Not tonight John Julian, I've got a meeting —I don't know if I'm ever going to get that 'Wendy House' ready for Thursday's assembly —and the Belle View Players need it for their rehearsals on Friday night- You know, Walter's play?"

"No, I didn't know he'd written a play. What's it called?"

"I thought everbody knew. It's called 'Scenes from a Wendy House'-It's about life in a primary school, we're all worried that it's going to be a send up of the school."

"Good! It needs a good send up!" He pauses and stares at the 'Wendy House', "Look leave it to me Allison. I'll make a start on the window frames tonight —Maybe I'll finish them. O.K?"

She walks up to him and kisses him primly on the forehead.

"Oh you're marvellous!"

"Thank you. Now what do I get if I paint the front door for you?"

She giggles, "You're impossible! I've got to fly. The paint's over there by my desk!" She skips out.

John Julian slowly and dejectedly takes off his jacket and dons the overall. He puts the classroom light on and switches the 'Wendy House' light off and begins painting. After a few minutes Brenda Gratten stalks in, cardigan around shoulders, smoking cloudfully.

"You've got red paint on your nose! –Where's Allison? Or shouldn't I ask?" She says cackling.

"She's just this minute gone –Is there much paint on my nose?"

"As long as you don't have it on your lips dear, you don't have to worry!" she cackles again, "Just a minute, what's she done with the white spirit?"

She rummages around and finds the bottle and an old rag nearby.

John Julian inspires, "White Spirit! Sounds like the ghost of Betty Teasdale!" He 'Uncle Toms' like mad, "Oh Great White Spirit, friend of dee African!..Take away dee black paint on my face!"

Brenda smokes and alternately cackles and coughs uncontrollably.

"Don't! Oh don't! You mustn't <u>say</u> that!" She dabs his face, "Oh it's worse now –Hold still!" He winces as she rubs harder and more successfully, "I can't bear that self righteous old cow. Why don't they send <u>her</u> to Africa instead of sending Jesus!" attempting to suppress her cackles.

"It would be too bloody expensive that's why. It's cheaper to send Jesus!"

"There! It's off! Want a ciggie?"

"Oh yes please! Do you mind if I carry on painting? –I promised Allison that I'd finish the windows tonight!"

"A labour of love is it dear? I'll light you up or try to!" she cackles again and lights his cigarette, "What I came for was my guillotine –Allison borrowed it!" She looks around with a mixture of suspicion and contempt.

John Julian seizing the comic edge, "Guillotine? I thought you were quite happy garroting miscreant children in your class Brenda!"

She renews her cackling, "You are awful. No, I just look at them and they - wilt!" suppressed cackles, "Ah here it is!" she picks it up and dangles it as she entertains her true thoughts, "look, can I possibly drag you round to dinner on Saturday night? The children are away in the Peak District this weekend, rock-climbing or pot-holing or something, so we thought we'd have small dinner party, a foursome –You could bring Allison if you like?"

"Oh honestly Brenda! Do you seriously think there's something going on between us? I'm old enough to be her grandfather –never mind father. Besides I hardly know the girl!"

"It's not what the oracle Mrs Teasdale's been saying!"

"What <u>has</u> that old witch been saying?"

"Don't be so touchy! Come by yourself then!"

John Julian winks, "Perhaps I'll bring Bulcastle! What do you think?"

"Don't mention that man's name to me again. If he came I'd poison the food. Which reminds me –<u>James</u> would like you to come aswell!" she cackles.

"As well as whom?"

"Me -You twit!"

"O.K. Done. I'll come by myself. How <u>is</u> James, by the way?"

"As you well know, James <u>is</u> as he has always been –an invalid. He gets better then he gets worse only to get better again etc etc. His condition is like the British weather –You never know quite what to expect next...You know, it's a terrible thing to say but I prefer him when he's ill —He's witty, amusing, alive —When he gets better he's such a dreadful bore. If he does finally get better, I shall divorce him..If he does finally get worse, I shall kill him unless nature does it for me!"

"Oh Brenda!!"

"Did I tell you we were due to fly to Bermuda last summer and then he fell ill again, we cancelled, and spent the most painfully amusing three weeks we've ever had together at the cottage —It rained every sodding day!" she puts the guillotine down and puts a hanky to her nose, "The boys get so fed up with him —we never see them most weekends. They don't come on holiday with us anymore. We're stuck with his mother most times we go away. You know she's ninety four —James was a somewhat unexpected present on her fortieth birthday —and she still goes on rambles and hikes. I think it's indecent for people to go on living to that age —especially when they're wealthy!" she half cries and half cackles and lights another cigarette, "Why is it that she's so fit and he's such a spastic? —She's buried two husbands!"

"Oh Brenda, don't torture yourself -and me!"

"Sorry love —I can't help it! Look we'll see you on Saturday..Tell you what, I'll pick you up myself at seven o'clock sharp. How's that!?"

"O.K. fine. Oh if you do decide to poison the food, don't let it be mine Brenda. I think I may have some useful life left in me that Barnside education Department might want to exploit."

Brenda resumes her happy cackle, "It'll be my food I'll be poisoning love if you don't turn up! See you!"

She quickly slobbers a kiss on his surprised but lifeless lips and scuttles out with the guillotine under one arm. He stares after her vacantly for a moment then resumes his painting. Bob Dredge shuffles in with his broom.

"I'm going to lock up now Mr Childs –Cos I've got to get off to a branch meeting!"

"I'm just about finished now Mr Dredge. Give me five minutes to clean up!"

"O.K. Mr Childs –Is that for Mr Sidebrother's play?"

"Oh you know about it too?"

"Oh yes. It's about this school, I think. The Belle View Players have been rehearsing in the evenings for the last three weeks. I'm surprised you don't know Mr Childs...It's going to cause a few upsets when it comes out..I think it's a comedy!" He exits, sweeping on the way.

John Julian chuckles to himself, "A comedy indeed! Now if I were to write a play about school, I'd be a bit more subtle. I'd call it 'The Wendy House' and it'd be a bloody tragedy!"

INTERLUDE 7

PARANOIA!

"DON'T LOOK AT ME DEAR READER! HE CREATED the word, our Walter Sidebrother –he of the gifted pen! Paranoia indeed! But there was a great deal to be paranoid about! The two of them were determined to get me as you will very soon see. Brenda Gratten and Betty Teasdale –my Scylla and Charybdis-have simply decided that I am to blame for all their woes and at every available opportunity they assail me. Don't listen to Walter, it has nothing to do with my function as Deputy head of this blighted establishment. They won't let me rest until they have put the boot in, or should I say 'high-heeled shoe'. Isn't it a bit pathetic that these two gargantuan oldish ladies should perch their senescent bodies on stilts like lusty young teenage girls?

But don't worry, I have my plans. They will get their come uppance, without Walter's literary permission thank you very much! Justice must be seen to be done and Walter does his best but I have plans of my own, you wait and see! Oh and please remember we are well into the term now, Christmas arrangements loom large, we're all tired, give us a break dear reader. We are teachers, with all the exhaustion and fatigue that the job entails, at the butt end of an autumn term, so give us a break!"

"May I say, as 'the Brenda Gratten' here being referred to in such a derogatory way that –I hardly recognise myself in this story to be honest-I've been a faithful devotee of 'Weight Watchers' for five years and more and I'm not a whisker over eight stones! It's criminal what he's been saying about me just now!!"

"May I say, as 'the Betty Teasdale' here being referred to in a slanderous manner, that I fully intend to speak to my solicitors about this little outburst! Walter tells the truth about him in the next scene and that's what he is so upset about so he wants to pass the buck to us. He should start behaving with the decorum that befits a Deputy Head and then maybe he would command more respect from the rest of us!"

"As the Deputy Head here being referred to, may I say I have nothing further to add except that I hope the reader will judge for himself from Walter's forthcoming scene!"

MORE STAFFROOM GAMES!

Lunchtime in the staffroom, a week later. Teachers sit at a large table eating slowly and silently. Mrs Teasdale sits at the head eating salad from a sandwich box clearly marked 'Mrs Teasdale'. Mr Childs sits at the other end unenthusiastically chewing school dinner. Brenda sits next to John Julian and Perdita sits next to Mrs Teasdale. Other members of staff sit around the staffroom reading and/or marking and drinking coffee/tea. Enter Walter with a school meal on a tray. He lets out a loud raspberry as he takes his place awkwardly between Brenda and Perdita mid-table.

Mrs Teasdale snaps, "Walter Sidebrother! Have you no manners at all? If you had any shame you'd leave the room instantly!"

"Shame on _you_ Mrs Teasdale, in some parts of the Upper Volta it is a hallowed custom betokening loyal affection between friends!"

Brenda sallies forth, "Loyal affection between consenting adults you mean – You are an old fart Walter. Settle down and eat your 'Beef Cobbler', perhaps it'll make a man of you and why are _you_ looking so disapprovingly John Julian? Don't tell me you're turning your nose up at our nutritionally- balanced school meals?"

John Julian picks at a morsel disdainfully before he replies, "I'm sure they're happier eaters in the Upper Volta. As for this, I've always been convinced that is one of the major contributory causes of cancer of the large bowel, but I've been eating the stuff for thirty years so I suppose some earnest young medical man with the dew of his Ph.D still fresh about his gills will tell me to stop eating soon."

Walter weighs in, "If the 'beef cobbler' gives you cancer as Mr Childs says, I wonder what the 'gooseberry fool' is going to give us!?"

Brenda sighs, "Don't tempt me Walter please!"

Mrs Teasdale opines, "I think everybody is taking too much for granted. You're all criticising the food but it doesn't stop you stuffing yourself with it!"

Brenda inspires, "Now that's something that might be worth trying Walter!"

"What?"

"Stuffing yourself with school dinner dear!"

Perdita interjects, "Oh Mrs Gratten, do you have to be so vulgar!"

John Julian tries to restore dignity to the occasion with a little light relief, he rises up and lifts his hands in mock despair!

"With the impossibility of school dinners on the one hand and the inevitability of Brenda's jokes on the other – I'm caught between Scylla and Charybdis!"

Brenda cackles, "How painful for you my dear – I hope you enjoy it!"

There is a metaphorical fanfare of trumpets as Walter attempts to dissipate the tension as he allows Brunhilde Waizmann to appear.

"Mr Bulcastle would like all record books in by the end of the week please (to murmurs of disapproval) and if you'd like to take note of tomorrow's menu: Cheese Salad followed by Chocolate mousse."

Walter breaks the awed silence, "Oh Brunhilde you make that menu sound like 'cordon bleu' –you won't forget the bottle of cold chablis will you?" Brunhilde imperiously rejoinders, "Just for you Walter!" She exits with a smile, a wink and great aplomb. Just as Avis enters (contrast in styles) struggling with a large goldfish bowl with two goldfish in it. She hyperventilates a complaint:

"There are two children standing outside Brunhilde's office And in point of fact they have been standing there for at least half an hour!"

Brenda, in between mouthfuls of 'beef cobbler', "Mark Starfield and Sanjeev Singh!"

"I think so, I just wondered why they were there that's all!" Avis exhales with a martyred sigh.

"They're there because they're there!"

"Oh, I see!" Not seeing, but feeling Brenda's malice, she backs down.

John Julian tackles heroically, "Somewhat cryptic from you Brenda? What have they been doing? Playing up in class? Not doing their homework? Failing to climb the North face of the Eiger in the allotted time?"

Brenda lashes out wildly, "Only extorting money out of Top Infant children that's all!! Try making a joke out of that one John Julian Childs!"

Perdita's conscience is roused, "How awful! The little ones bring in their money for Mrs Teasdale's 'Send Jesus to Africa' fund and those Junior louts waylay them. I'm glad you're not letting them get away with anything Mrs Gratten. There's too much laxity in the school as it is. Bulcastle is no help. These days he spends all his time in his room studying holiday brochures and whenever we send children to him for discipline, he shows them pictures of the Swiss Alps. What <u>can</u> you do!? The school is going to pot!"

Mrs Teasdale, eyes swivelling to notice the hovering Avis:

"Avis, <u>do</u> put down that goldfish bowl and sit down for a while!"

"I've got the Middle Infants Creative Maths Group in ten minutes –I haven't the time. If only there were more than twenty four hours in a day!", head cocked patronisingly on one side, "Hurry Hilary! We begin in ten minutes!" She blusters out, goldfish bowl precariously under one arm, clipboard in the other. John Julian adds:

"..And if there <u>were</u> more than twenty four hours in a day, she'd still fill those extra hours with education! Creative Maths indeed! What's 'creative' about Maths? 2+2=4 What do you do? Do you make it '5' for fun?"

Hilary rising up with irritation, "You're only showing your educational ignorance Mr Childs, as per usual!"

She exits with an identical bowl to Avis but with <u>three</u> goldfish in it!

John Julian, hands up in mock despair, "I only ask cos I want to know!"

Perdita intervenes, "Why do we always get sidetracked in this staffroom? The point we should be discussing is how we can stop the rising tide of violence, vandalism and general bad manners in this school!"

"You're beginning to sound like a well-known daily newspaper Perdita, the one I saw you reading only this morning!"

Mrs Teasdale defends Perdita, "Cynicism doesn't help Mr Childs! If only we had adequate, <u>inspired</u> leadership at Belle View School, these problems would not arise!" Perdita adds her 'hear hears!'

Allison, having finished with her nails, rises suddenly –transfixed!

"Those were <u>my</u> goldfish they just went off with! <u>My</u> goldfish! Mr Benson from the Environmental Projects Section brought them. They were earmarked for my 'Wildlife Corner'! They're always taking things for their 'Creative Maths Group'! First it was my coloured pegs and my activity balls and <u>now</u> my goldfish!" She stamps out petulantly.

Walter chips in with an American accent, "It's a never-ending drama, folks, at Belle View School!"

Brenda doesn't respond to Walter's 'funnies' but is anxious to target John Julian and gently leads him into her conversational trap:

"Talking about 'Drama'. If Mr Bottomly is taking Liz's class for P.E., Hilary is going on her 'Engineering for Infants' course at the Poly and Joyce is away sick <u>again</u> –How are you going to take my class for Drama this afternoon Mr Childs? You can't use the hall anyway remember?"

John Julian deflects with some humorous throat-clearing "Well-erhmm!"

But Brenda is relentless, "And also remember that we've been told that we can't have anymore supply teachers as we've already got one for Joyce's class and Bulcastle told Brunhilde only yesterday that with the cutbacks and everything they're putting their foot down on unnecessary supplies. Well?" John Julian continues his throat-clearing antic, "Well... erhmm..yes!"

Perdita defends, "Leave the poor man alone can't you see he's having his lunch?"

"He <u>is</u> Deputy Head Perdita dear –that's what he's paid to sort out and I want to plan for this afternoon's lessons!"

"It sounds as though you've already sorted it out yourself

Brenda. No extra supply teachers so I've got to take Hilary's class and you'll just have to miss Drama unless <u>you</u> take Hilary's class and forfeit your free period for the greater good of Belle View School?"

"Couldn't you split Hilary's class Mr Childs? –and then you'd be free to take mine?"

Mrs Teasdale butts in, "Brenda, why don't you do as he says and take Hilary's class. We've all got to make compromises in this world and why should the children suffer?"

Brenda explodes! "Why should I give up my free period because of Barnside Education Authority's incompetence!! They've known for three bloody months that Hilary was going on that course!"

John Julian wet blankets, "But they couldn't have foreseen that Joyce was going to be ill that's the trouble!"

Mrs Teasdale calls a halt, "Leave it to Howard Bulcastle to sort things through!"

Brenda, agitated to the point of dementia, "He's senile! He couldn't sort his way through a paper bag! I'm fed up with this bloody school!" She gets up and stands near the window, lights a cigarette and looks out.

There is a peace for a little while. Mrs Teasdale leaves the table and settles down to her knitting, sitting in her favourite chair that Walter has quickly vacated.

Perdita also starts her knitting, "Did you know that Alice Tweedsmuir is going to have another baby?"

Radcliffe stops reading and looks over her specs, "I didn't know that!!"

"Yes, she told me this morning on the way school –I always give her a lift on Tuesdays."

"That's five she's got isn't it? Or is it six?"

"Six, I wonder if it'll be another boy!?"

Walter, with a male's impatience with conversational trivia, calls out:

"And who the hell's Alice Tweedsmuir, when she's at home?"

Perdita dismissively, "Walter really, go back to sleep! She's an Infant dinner lady, the one who covers the bottom playground!"

"That's Boofie? Are they one and the same person?" Walter asks innocently. Brenda inhaling rapidly and blowing out aggressively, "Oh God! There must be something else apart from this dump –if only someone could point it out to me!!"

Mrs Teasdale sermonises without looking up from her knitting:

"That's a horrible thing to say Mrs Gratten and I'm sure you're only saying that because you are a little overwrought. Life is what you make it!"

John Julian responds, "Strike while the iron is hot! Make hay while the sun shines! (Brenda cackles) Every cloud has a silver lining! It's a long lane that has no turning! It is an ill wind that blows nobody any good! Plenty of advice there Brenda –Take your pick!"

Mrs Teasdale, visibly annoyed, "John Julian you should never have gone in for teaching! Cynicism and Education don't go together!"

"........It's no use locking the stable door after the horse has bolted! Look before you leap!...Don't put all your eggs in one basket and if by some misfortune you happen to do so, don't count your chickens before they're hatched!" Brenda is in hysterics by this time.

Perdita pours a little cold moral water on things, "Will you all stop now! I think we should all try to be happy. We have a duty to be happy for the children's sake!"

"'Thou shalt be happy'! My God!" whispers Brenda staring despairingly. Allison returns, having calmed down and freshened up, she makes her contribution, "Yes! We have a duty to be happy for our own sakes!"

Perdita beams at the unexpected support, "Very true Allison! 'Out of the mouths of babes and sucklings!'"

John Julian, looking in vain for allies, "Radcliffe! You haven't made a contribution to this pool of wisdom!"

"Well, I don't think I really want to! (continuing with her knitting –yes she is a knitter too!) You can't talk about life can you, you've just got to get on with it as best you may and happiness is a sort of by-product of it all, which can't be morally legislated for I would have thought Mrs Teasdale?"

"Radcliffe Ball! You're one of life's innocents, and that's my last word on the subject!" snaps Mrs Teasdale contemptuously clicking her knitting needles even louder than is strictly necessary for the completion of her husband's sweater.

John Julian not wanting Mrs Teasdale to have the last moral word:

"Well now that we have finally resolved the fundamental mysteries of the universe, could we move on to the much more serious matter of school stock. We appear to be very short of shiny paper, coloured pencils and paint. So could you all go easy for the rest of this term until we get fresh supplies. I put a Z order in this morning and she should have these items by early next term."

Mrs Teasdale mustering more indignation than is required:

"But that's _after_ Christmas!! What's everyone going to use for Christmas art work? This is ridiculous Mr Childs!!"

Perdita joins the bandwagon: "Didn't I say the school was going to pot! Imagine a school without coloured pencils and crayons!"

"I'm <u>sorry</u> but I <u>have</u> put in the Z order and marked it urgent! I can't do anymore!"

Brenda, in emotional crescendo, "God! If you just did your job properly and anticipated a little, we might be able to avoid these endless stock crises and the accompanying nervous breakdowns! You <u>are</u> becoming a bore John Julian!"

"No, just down to earth Brenda! Paint and coloured pencils are the very lifeblood of the school! (he laughs at his own preposterous tone)..Oh God this place must be getting to me. I can't sleep at nights you know – I get all this – this stock rubbish floating up into my consciousness!"

Mrs Teasdale conversationally triumphing, "Stock <u>is</u> a serious business! I'm glad you're taking something seriously for a change John Julian!"

Allison, running to his defence, "He's taking it <u>too</u> seriously! It's giving him nightmares!"

"Well, if it wasn't school stock it would be something else Allison- I'm one of life's worriers alas!"

Perdita perks up as she opens up her copy of the 'Daily Telegraph':

"Try to look on the bright side Mr Childs!"

John Julian bursts out laughing, "I try to Perdita but my ulcers keep dragging me back into the shadows. I need to escape. Perhaps I should be a missionary and go to Africa to tell the natives that they've a duty to be happy!"

Mrs Teasdale rallies, "Ah but you'd need to believe in something first before you go out there Mr Childs!"

"Oh no! That would be a handicap Betty! It would be the quickest way to the cooking pot! I'd just tell them to keep on believing what they believed in, but I would encourage them to see the advantage of flush toilets and other modern amenities!"

"Why do you have to drag everything down to your own coarse level!!??"

"Oh you know why Betty. Why tempt providence by asking??"

Perdita mercifully intervenes, "Take no notice of him Mrs Teasdale. He enjoys pulling people's legs!"

At this point Howard Bulcastle enters the staffroom:

"Can I have your attention please! Bruno Busby has been doing something unpleasant in beakers and he's just thrown a 'beef cobbler' at Mrs Hunningford...He's in your class Mrs Gratten so I'd be obliged if you dealt with it!...I've got a Head teachers' meeting and I must be off now. I won't be back this afternoon Mr Childs."

He exits as Brenda Gratten rises, fag in mouth, bag on shoulder:

"Typical! He passes the buck whenever he has the opportunity! Head teachers' meeting my foot! That's the third one he's had this past month, to my knowledge!" she slowly exits and on the way puts her cigarette out in Walter's coffee saucer –giving him a sidelong wink, "Didn't know that Heads liked each other that much!" she cackles.

Walter responds, "..And 'beef cobbler' to you too Brenda!"

As she exits she pops her head back round the door and wrinkles her nose at him. Allison discreetly closes the door properly and half-whispers:

"I noticed that Mr Bulcastle had his golf clubs on the back seat of his car this morning...I wonder!"

"Yours is not to wonder about the doings of your elders and betters Miss Allison –Just go and do your dinner duty – I think you've forgotten love!"

"Oh God! Sorry Mr Childs!" She exits promptly.

"If there isn't as teacher down there promptly in future I

can see them throwing Mrs Hunningford let alone the 'beef cobbler'-that fourth year are getting a bit out of hand. Still, Brenda'll put the fear of God into them!..Talking about God. How much money have you raised so far for your 'Send Jesus to Africa' fund Betty?"

"I don't really know whether I want to talk to you Mr Childs, unless you are being serious and not looking for an opportunity to poke fun!"

"Obviously not much money, say no more!"

"As a matter of fact it is coming in, albeit slowly - £17-29 to date!"

"That wouldn't send Jesus much further than the Blackwall tunnel! I don't know about darkest Africa!"

"There's plenty more money committed that hasn't yet come in. Try having some faith John Julian Childs, the Lord will provide. Incidentally Radcliffe, how is that mural coming on? It was good of Howard Bulcastle to give you the whole of the back wall in the hall. I'm really looking forward to seeing it, it will set the seal so to speak on all I've tried to do in this school since I came so many years ago."

"I took a peek at it last night. It's most interesting and unusual I'd say." Perdita, angrily rejoinders, "You're not supposed to see it Allison!! No one is, until it is complete and officially unveiled on the last day of term! Even Mrs Teasdale hasn't seen it and it's dedicated to her achievements!"

Mrs Teasdale, blushing and knitting even faster, "I don't know about 'achievements' but it's nice of you to say that Perdita. But please don't tell anyone what you've seen Allison, it'll spoil it for the children and us. We want it to be a surprise!"

Radcliffe explains, "I want it to be a nice surprise Mrs Teasdale. I've put a lot into it (murmurs of agreement) – The theme of 'Jesus in Africa' was a difficult one and there's still lots more to do but I expect I'll be finished by early December."

Hilary burst in with a clatter and a bang:

"Please! Someone! Anyone! Give us a hand! Meena Ramjit has wet herself all over Avis's floral Maths display in the New Hall! I've got Philip Burston in tears because Agnes Rowcroft has been colouring in his project book by mistake, or so he says, and Avis has got her hands full with Mrs Swanage who's rabbiting on about free balloons for the over seventies at the Christmas Fair! Please will someone come! We'll just have to pack up Creative Maths at lunchtime that's all, I can't cope anymore!"

Radcliffe calmly deals with her, "Wait a minute love, I'll give you a hand and at least stem the tide of Meena Ramjit -she always was a waterworks and her brother was just the same! It must be 'culture shock', the family being kicked out of Uganda like that –It's enough to make anyone wet their knickers!"

Radcliffe follows a distraught Hilary through the door.

Perdita puts away her knitting and follows them out, raising her eyebrows to John Julian, "I suppose I'd better see what all the fuss is about!"

John Julian is left alone in the staffroom with Mrs Teasdale, he muses:

"What busy lives we lead at Belle View School! I think I'll go and have a quiet smoke in the school garden!" he goes towards the door.

"That won't solve anything! Smoking will shorten your life and it's a bad example to the children Mr Childs and you know it is!"

"Yes, well, there are two good reasons for carrying on the habit I suppose. But actually I'm smoking for purely selfish, personal reasons Betty. I just happen to enjoy doing it. It is one of the few pleasures remaining to me in my declining years. <u>You</u> have religion –I have tobacco, and long may we both prosper!" He exits just as Avis's clock goes off yet again.

"Damn that cuckoo clock!" Mrs Teasdale fumes.

INTERLUDE 8

Radcliffe's Mural

" **J**OHN JULIAN BACK AGAIN .. 'I LIFT UP MINE EYES TO THE hills whence cometh my help'. The psalmist must have been thinking of me when he wrote those words and maybe he was anticipating those rolling hills in Radcliffe's mural. So let me rewrite those holy words in a modern, traumatically modern context. 'I lift up mine eyes to the 'mural' from whence cometh my help'. You see folks, Radcliffe, dear innocent but imaginative Radcliffe Ball has done it all for me. You haven't seen her mural? You have a treat in store. I took a look at it last night. But I won't spoil the fun and tell you all. Read on to learn the wonderful horror of it all. Put it this way, it may very well send Jesus to Africa but it will indubitably send Elizabeth Barratt Teasdale completely round the theological twist! There is a God after all and he has sent his servant Radcliffe Ball to administer his justice –without any human intervention from me. Look! No hands! Now if he could see his divine way clear to meting out a similar retribution on Mrs Brenda Gratten he will have me down on my knees praising His name, quick as a lightning flash................... No such luck so far, but if it could be arranged, Oh Lord, you would not only get my heartfelt thanks but also my name on the credal dotted line! Now on to the next little chapter in Walter's every day story of teaching folk, ugh! Here is Walter parading his own little literary devices at their most crass and obvious and revealing himself too well.

YET MORE WENDY HOUSE GAMES!

It is after school some days later, about five thirty. John Julian and Walter are finishing off painting the Wendy

House, putting the finishing touches to the window frames and the door —with Allison watching.

Allison is on the point of going, she gives last minute instructions before she leaves: "Oh and could you put the hooks up inside for the curtains? – Thank you chaps –I've got to fly now!" she exits as John Julian and Walter watch on in disappointment. John Julian breaks the ice:

"The original intention was just to <u>help</u> her with this –We seem to be doing it all Walter!"

"Yes, she has a w-w-way of getting p-people to d-d-d-do things for her! I was very w-w-willing to do things for her, but painting her W-Wendy House wasn't what I had in mind!"

"Walter you surprise me! You wanted to have your wicked way with her, didn't you?"

"Well, you m-must admit that she's a b-bit of all right. Now come on, don't play the 'elder statesman-rising-above-it-all' with me! You tried as well Mr Childs –admit it!"

"Don't be so vulgar Walter. What are you suggesting? That I, a middle-aged man, with the position of Deputy Head Teacher, should wantonly and unashamedly try to take advantage of a young probationary teacher barely out of college?"

"Y-yes, in short!"

"Such wicked and lubricious thoughts hardly ever rise above the surface of my mind –hardly ever anyway (Walter sniggers).. but enough of this wild talk. I want to know about this play of yours that the Belle View Players are putting on. The rumour going round is that it is all about us!"

"Not really. The whole idea of the play is to have adults playing the p-parts of children. There won't be any teachers in it, it's just a play about children in school. If there is a point to the play it is to show how children are very much like adults in the way they relate to each other in their lives at school." There's a pause in the conversation.

"It doesn't sound very convincing to me Walter. But if the Belle View Players are taking it on there must be some redeeming features somewhere. For my part, I'm not very interested in children and their ways. That's why I am in teaching I suppose –a kind of divine retribution, law of karma and all that. I see my job as trying to change each little monster into some semblance of an adult –Horrible big adults being somehow preferable to horrible little children, in my view!"

"I think I prefer ch-ch-children really. Are you saying you don't like children Mr Childs?"

"No, I didn't say that Walter. Of course I like children, who doesn't? It's a simple taste, simple to acquire, like liking sweets, cakes, lemonade etc. What I object to are people who make out that children are more interesting than they actually are –investing them with some pure, pristine imagination that gets spoilt as they get older. This is nonsense. Children have no imagination until adults open it up for them. God knows I ought to know, having taught Art and Music for thirty years. Of course, the 'naïve' school of art must not be underestimated but then it is naïve and it is only art because adults have dignified it as a style and raised it the level of art. Sermon over. Amen!"

"Oh I think children have p-p-powerful imaginations that are spoilt by b-bad teachers who b-b-bully and cajole them into b-b-believing in things about themselves and others that are n-n-not true! B-b-bother, I've dropped paint on my shoe!"

"Ooh, do I detect a chip on somebody's shoulder? -There's a rag and white spirit behind you- and let me guess the name of this 'chip'-Mrs Teasdale!"

"G-G-God forbid! Th-That's your child Mr Chips –sorry, I mean your chip Mr Childs!"

"I'm willing to bet house points that she's in your play!"

"N-No I told you. There are no teachers in my play at all –only their victims, the children!"

"Well, it's a moot point as to who is the executioner and who the condemned, in our educational system Walter –pass me the rag, I've smudged something here –Personally if I wrote a play about school, I'd give Betty Teasdale the starring part in my very realistic drama. It would be settling a very old score!"

"Maybe she'd like to write a play about you!"

"I daresay, and her play would be a comedy no doubt with me and thee at the butt end of it. But my play –pass me the rag again- would be a tragedy with a very interesting denouement!"

"What would you call it? 'Murder in the Stock Cupboard'?"

"Nothing as cleverly trite as that Walter. I'd call my play 'The Wendy House'! –Stark, simple and oh so truly tragic!"

"B-But you can't. My play is called 'Scenes From a Wendy House' –I got there first!"

"So what! My play would be just that bit more subtle and realistic –in any case it would have no children in it at all, only teachers."

"How can you have a school without children?"

"How can you have a school without teachers? Except, where the teachers are like children themselves....Oh I'm gibbering. A day at school makes me gibber –normally I gibber to myself but you happen to be here Walter sorry. What time is it?" (looks at his watch)

"Tell me what happens at the end of your p-p-play?"

"But it hasn't been written yet..In any case it would

spoil things if I did tell you. Just wait and see. I'm more interested in the ending of your play Walter, which is, after all, complete."

"The ch-ch-children discover that they are playing games just like the adults and since they are <u>just</u> games they suddenly realise that the rules can be changed to suit them."

"Sounds very heavy and intellectual to me. Are you <u>sure</u> it's a comedy? It sounds very serious and philosophical (wipes his hands on rag and gets up with a grunt from his semi-recumbent position) You won't get many people from the Belle View Estate interested in philosophy!"

"No it's not in the least like 'philosophy' –It's much more live than that and down to earth. You must c-c-come and see it. W-we're putting it on on the last evening of term, about a week before Christmas!"

"It'll be Betty Teasdale's last day at school and the unveiling of Radcliffe's mural. That'll be enough excitement for her for one day, I doubt she'll want to come and see your play as well!"

"I shall certainly invite her."

"It must be quite harmless then! You're a good man Walter Sidebrother, I'm the one with the chip on my shoulder –or I'm the Mr Chips with Mrs Teasdale on one shoulder and Brenda Gratten on the other! (wearily) I must go. Tidy up for me would you?"

"Oh are you g-going so soon Mr Childs? I was going to buy you a drink and you were going to give me as lift home remember? There's a pub over Hampstead way called the 'Bears Hotel' –Know it?"

"Mrs Teasdale lives just opposite that pub. It's the Belle View Arms for us tonight Walter lad. See you by the car!" John Julian exits.

INTERLUDE 9

Plots and Plans!

"JOHN JULIAN AGAIN...A CHAP HAS GOT TO MAKE SENSE of his life hasn't he? Specially when you hit the fifties and you know there's a hell of a lot more behind you than in front of you! Brenda's been annoying me again. She got into one of her moods —one minute she's up in the air saying she misses me and needs me etc and the next minute she's down and angry and threatening to tell the authorities about our grubby little affair which she reckons was, I quote, 'conducted in lieu of paid time allocated for school business' whatever that means. She really is the end. I told her, point one —nobody could possibly be interested in our grubby little gropings which were done on my private property —and the Science syllabus was completed on time anyway, point two —if she thinks that by passing on this info' to the local authority she will jeopardise whatever slim chances I may have for promotion, then good luck-I have never had any ambitions for Headship! Of course she got a little cross at being thus thwarted and stormed out of my office to give the kids in her class the benefit of her wrath.

As for the other 'chip' on my shoulder, Betty Teasdale. She is constantly spying on me these days, and this is not just my natural paranoia. Only last week I caught her peering through Allison's classroom window —I pretended to hide in the Wendy House and she just glared at Allison and then at me. Yesterday in the staffroom, she point blank accused me of taking an advanced peek at Radcliffe's mural. Now why would I want to do that? I told her I'd rather watch paint dry! She then said I was being insulting. She ignores me now and cold shoulders me at every available opportunity – which suits me fine.

But there is a pocket of warmth and comfort in my soul —darling Allison is getting friendlier by the day but I won't bore you with all the grubby details —frankly, it's none of your business dear reader and I'm going to leave it to your imagination. Oh I am a tease aren't I? Just follow the next couple of episodes and you'll learn to read between the lines, I hope.

One final thought......perish the thought!

CHRISTMAS IN THE STAFFROOM (NOTICE THE DECORATIONS!)

Yes, it <u>is</u> Christmas now and <u>do</u> notice the lovely decorations and the tinsel round the window! You can just about hear the strains of a children's choir in the distance, 'Old King Wenceslas' wending his weary way from the Old Hall! The women members of the staff all sit round knitting –surprise, surprise! The male members sit round drinking coffee and staring into space. They should all be sitting in a semi-circle, waiting for the party games to begin. Avis Gunn comes in looking harassed as ever!

"Has anyone seen my 'Star of Bethlehem'? It's been in Mrs Goldberg's family for generations and if we've lost it, I don't think I'll ever be able to attend another P.T.A. meeting again! It's irreplaceable!"

Brenda, smokes and exhales fiercely as though the pressure of a busy term has to be relieved through someone –Avis is the first victim:

"Oh come off it Avis Gunn! Nothing's irreplaceable and that includes us! If Barnside Education Authority have their way, you'll be lucky to still have your job never mind a bloody 'Star of Bethlehem'!"

Radcliffe commiserates, "I'll give you a hand Avis. It's probably in that cupboard in the Art Room where the Drama stuff is kept- I'll go and see." Mrs Teasdale, after two pearl and one plain, "Look stop it both of you! Sit down and rest! (They both stop in their tracks) This is our break time and we're all entitled to forget school just for fifteen minutes surely!"

Hilary supports joyously, "That's the first sensible thing I've heard all day. Bulcastle has been in and out of my classroom like a yo yo with petty complaints about the decorations in the library <u>and</u> my piano playing. Brunhilde has been driving me nuts all day about the schedules for the Nativity Play! Roll on Christmas!"

Walter joins in the festive cheer, "It's precisely one week, three days and four and a half hours. What <u>I'm</u> trying to work out is the connection between Rachel Goldberg and the 'Star of Bethlehem'"

Brenda explodes, "She's Jewish! you cretin!"

"That's precisely my point Brenda. What's a Jew doing with the 'Star of Bethlehem'? I thought they didn't believe in it!"

"My God! Haven't you ever heard of the Star of David. You know, that little yellow job that Uncle Adolf had embroidered on their pyjamas! Christ!" Brenda jumps up to make herself more coffee –cackling hysterically.

Mrs Teasdale intervenes, "Brenda, I really wish you would calm down and stop being so rude to everyone. We know that you're tired after that magnificent Open Evening display that you organised, but we're all tired at this time of the year!"

John Julian, stirring the pot gently, "Mind you, Brenda's right in a way. The Jews do believe in the Star, it's just that they didn't see the one everyone else saw over the stable in Bethlehem!"

Allison, sniggering delightfully, "Oh you are a card Mr Childs! Incidentally, did you say you'd try to get me some of that gold sugar paper and the spirit masters? I've asked Mr Bulcastle until I'm blue in the face and all he says is yes and does nothing!"

John Julian (hopes rising), "Allison, I'm just plasticine in your hands!" Radcliffe and Avis unfreeze and, like the Magi before them, go about their search for that elusive Star,

"Come on Avis, let's go find that Star!" She breaks into song, "'We three Kings of Orient are..' Haven't you even had your coffee yet?"

"You know I never eat or drink when I'm teaching Radcliffe. Just let me banda off some worksheets <u>and</u> I'll be with you in a jiff."

John Julian gets up, pops a paper crown on his head (Tony Budd made it in Class 3) and bars their exit!

"No wait! You two bring the Gold and the Frankincense and I'll bring the myrrh!"

Avis, head on one side with a wan smile, "Oh you are a wag Mr Childs but it won't get me my Star! Come along Radcliffe love, ignore him!"

The two of them exit. Julian makes himself another coffee and returns to his seat.

"Those two women are martyrs to education!"

Mrs Teasdale starts up, "At least they take things seriously Mr Childs!" Brenda, in seismic seizure, "Oh! He <u>doesn't</u> take things seriously, is that the implication? He's been here for twenty odd years and he's in deadly earnest Mrs Teasdale. You are looking forward to retiring with your husband to that little cottage in Morecambe Bay with roses down the wall. He already lives in a cottage like that and he's <u>not</u> looking forward to his retirement. We can't <u>all</u> have our prayers answered Mrs Teasdale!"

Brenda struts out muttering and slams the door behind her.

Hilary, open-mouthed, "What was all that in aid of?"

John Julian sighs, "Brenda does like to carry other people's crosses as well as her own. I only wish she'd let me do my own suffering, it's so much easier to bear when it's <u>not</u> shared!"

An irate Mrs Teasdale responds, "That's a blasphemous thing to say Mr Childs! The Lord Jesus will bear all our burdens for us if only we go to Him in a spirit of penitence and humility!"

Perdita unbridles her Catholicism, "You may not be gifted with the <u>true</u> faith Mrs Teasdale but, for once, I agree with you wholeheartedly!"

"..One Lord, one faith, one baptism Perdita!"

"...And <u>one</u> headmaster, to whom I am going, in a spirit of penitence and humility, for some gold sugar paper and banda spirit masters. O.k. Allison?" John Julian goes to the door.

Allison blows him a kiss. "You're an angel"

"That's the nicest things anyone has said to me all day –Allison, you're in grave danger of getting five team points <u>and</u> a gold star!"

He exits on cloud nine!

Mrs Teasdale is furious, "That man's a pernicious influence in this school!" Perdita smugly defends him, "No, no Mrs Teasdale! He's just pulling your leg a little. He's misguided that's all! He's an atheist, but he means well!" Allison angrily rebuts this, "I think that's a patronising thing to say Miss O'Toole! I don't think that any label quite fits John Julian Childs. He's got a heart of gold and the children love him!"

Mrs Teasdale, primly continuing with her knitting, "I'm not talking about him as a person. I'm talking about his beliefs!"

"I can't really see how you can separate the two!"

Hilary pretends to creep out –just as Avis bursts in.

"I've found my gold star!! You'll never guess where it was?? Only behind Howard Bulcastle's filing cabinet under a pile of 'Gunpowder Plot' worksheets and a whole mountain of half-woven raffia baskets!"

Mrs Teasdale clucking, "Howard does like his basket-weaving!"

Avis, losing her cool, "That's not the point Mrs Teasdale! If it hadn't been for Radcliffe Ball's searching gaze, I might never have got it back –and do you know what else we found there?? I can't bring myself to think about it! We found my 'Toddlers' Time' Reading Schedules that I thought I had mislaid and he had them all the time! It took me three months to work those out and I had to do them all again!"

Walter pipes up, "Those 'Gunpowder Plot' worksheets are mine Avis!"

Brunhillde Waizmann enters majestically (Christmas musical background changes to Wagner's 'Ride of the Valkyries') and maintains her dignity in utterance in spite of recent slights:

"Telephone call for you Walter- Chess match I think. It's Mr Braysworthy from Blessed Innocents School.......... There's a parent to see you Allison -Mrs Patel, she's worried about the amount of plasticine Arvid is taking home in his pockets, apparently he's got a whole bedroom full of it. (Allison leaves quickly).......One final message from on high -Mr Bulcastle wants to start his basket weaving periods with the Upper Juniors straight after Christmas please!" She sails out full-sailed and glorious.

Mrs Teasdale comments, "What did I say? He does like his basketry!"

Brenda Gratten re-enters carrying a pile of books to be marked. The staffroom quietens in anticipation of further squalls to come.

"We all know what THAT means Walter! Water on the floor, canes on the floor, baskets in the sink, nothing finished and bloody chaos everywhere!"

Mrs Teasdale gingerly replies, "At least he does take classes. Many heads can't be bothered!"

"Basket weaving!! It's the educational equivalent to sewing mailbags -I'd rather he stayed out of my classroom!" with that Brenda sits on the edge of her seat and smokes nervously.

Walter exits for the phone, firing a passing shot as he does: "Hear! Hear! If you can't do it, teach it! And if you can't can't teach it b-b-b-become a headmaster."

Perdita steps in, "Ah no no! Stop it! All of you! The poor man can't help being an old fool! He does his best! He means well!"

Brenda wades in, "Perdita! You seem to think good intentions are enough, they're not. Why should we put up with his incompetence! He should have been put out to grass years ago! He's a menace that man!"

Mrs Teasdale tries to restore calm, "Now that's not fair Brenda! He's done a lot of good for the school- those camping holidays in Scotland for the fourth years, the new pottery kiln, and he did persuade Mr Blackstone to go for early retirement when none of us thought he would EVER go."

Perdita, hackles rising, "Seamus Blackstone was a very nice man! His people were from Cork!"

"He was a pervert! I don't call that nice! He couldn't keep his hands to himself. He was always being over affectionate towards the children, giving them sweets and presents. I wasn't natural," said Mrs Teasdale.

Avis, on a perch at long last, tweets innocently," Seamus was a damn good teacher and he loved the children. He NEVER did anything unnatural!"

"Unless you call putting your hand up someone's skirt unnatural! He tried it on me once in the library!" Brenda observes, cackling mischievously.

Perdita adamantly defends the man from Cork, "Well I don't believe it!"

"Yes he did! I was on the little step-ladder, looking up 'Mountains and Rivers' for a Geography lesson when I found that HE was looking up ME!"

"Disgusting! What did I tell you!!" triumphes Mrs Teasdale.

"Yes! And then he started doing a bit of exploring and he'd got halfway up my left thigh when he could see that I was enjoying myself and he sort of lost confidence! They're all the same these perverts when you play them at their own game -Harmless! If you'll excuse me I've got a quick phone call to make, if Walter can be persuaded to get off that phone. He's a phone fetishist that man!" she exits cackling.

The room is alive with clicking needles as the guardians of morality assess Mrs Gratten's performance. Mrs Teasdale kicks off followed closely by Miss O'Toole:

"That woman is disgusting! She's got a mind like a sewer!"

"You must admit that she's a very good teacher though! Keeps good order in her classroom and her room is as clean and tidy as a new pin!"

Avis concludes, "My God!! There's only only one answer to THAT!"

She stomps out with a backward petulant stare at her elders and betters!

At this point we really ought to have the 'Cuckoo Clock' going off once again but Avis has alas mislaid it again.

INTERLUDE 10

Oh Yes! The High Point of my Little Life!

"VERY DOG HAS ITS DAY! AND WALTER HAS faithfully preserved some semblance of that wonderful day when my growling fantasies about Allison actually met with some reality for a change (there IS a God!), only you have to substitute the Wendy House for the dog kennel......a little more romantic perhaps but there is the hint of comedy!

I really don't want to say anymore. Over to you Walter...

A CHRISTMAS WENDY HOUSE!
(NOTICE THE MISTLETOE!)

It is about five o'clock on the day before school breaks up for the Christmas holidays. Allison's classroom is festooned with decorations and balloons. But the room is in darkness except for the Wendy House, lit up like Aladdin's cave in which a tinsel-crowned Allison sits marking books. There is also a small Christmas tree in the corner with its flickering blossoms of coloured lights.

Bob Dredge, about his duties, sweeps his way in, "Is that you in there Miss Prestatyn?"

"Of course it is Mr Dredge. Who do you think it was?"

"I was just wondering if you'd finished your 'Leaf Collecting Club' so I could do a bit of sweeping like ..Get it?"

"Yes, I do get it Bob! As a matter of fact I was just marking a few books. I know it's a bit late but could you come back in say half an hour?"

"I'm due to lock up at five thirty tonight you know –but I'll stretch a point seeing as it's you Allison! You don't mind if I call you 'Allison' seeing as it's Christmas?"

"I'll stretch a point Bob –seeing as it's you! See you later"

Bob sweeps his way out and shortly afterwards Walter

Sidebrother comes in wearing a paper hat and carrying a bottle and two glasses.

"You there Allison?"

She opens wide the door of the Wendy House.

"Well, it's not Betty Teasdale! What are you doing here? I thought Chess finished at half four?"

"Shut up and hold these glasses!"

Walter wobbles and sits down awkwardly beside her and, in the way of all conscientious drunks, carefully pours the drinks out so they have exactly equal amounts in their glasses.

"Look, I want to finish marking these books so that I can go out tonight. Please Walter!"

"Oh come on Allison! It's Christmas! Show a bit of seasonal joy!"

"You've spilt that sherry all over Bertram Target's Handwriting Book-You are a nuisance!"

"Walter peers at the book, "Well judging by Bertram Target's writing efforts sherry is too good for him! I can think of a more appropriate liquid with which to b-b-baptise his efforts!" He pauses to drink, "Anyway, it's not sherry, it's brandy. Try some!"

He wobbles a glass at her.

"I can't!"

"Oh go on, just one glass!" she relents and downs it in one go and then stares suggestively at him, Walter wilts, "M-My God! I d-didn't think you were like that Allison P-Prestatyn! You can certainly p-p-put it away!"

"Mrs Teasdale would not approve Walter! It's not the right sort of spirit for this time of the year!"

"Don't mention the name of that awful woman again, it's Christmas!

There's not much room in here thank goodness –Give us a kiss for Christmas Miss!"

He slobbers across to her but she can see that he is drunk and incapable, so she fobs him off –firmly but with humour.

"I think you're drunk Walter and to think you took a club activity as well!"

"D-Don't you ever listen to Bulcastle's notices –the comprehensible ones that is- I cancelled it you twit, so that I could go to the teachers' centre party! W-W-When I found that you weren't there, I thought I'd mosey on back here where I thought you'd be!"

"Don't you _ever_ give up Walter? Anyway, I thought you and Brenda had something going after that fourth year camping holiday in Scotland."

"B-B-Brenda!? You must be joking! One night with Brenda and I'd be talking with a high voice for the rest of m-m-my life. Besides, the only thing she really enjoys is pulling off the w-w-w-wings of children. S-See, it's brought my stammer b-b-back!"

"Poor you!"

"W-Why does everyone have to feel sorry for me all the time! I don't want p-p-pity Allison! I just want a g-g-g-good screw, but I don't seem able to p-p-persuade anyone to comply. The only mating I ever seem able to do is b-b-b-bloody stale-mating! My b-b-bishop gets in the way of my m-mating queen! Here I go talking chess again!"

"You should try to relax more Walter, and _try_ to stop thinking of _yourself_ all the time –it's not a very attractive quality! You're a very nice boy and I'm sure you'll meet the right girl one of these days."

"I'm thirty five Allison! Time's running out –I shall probably end up with a mature widow like Mrs Parkfield who wants someone to mother!"

"Mrs Parkfield <u>isn't</u> a widow!"

"It isn't for want of trying though is it? She's already chosen the hospital for his final illness and I expect she's got the gravedigger on standby!"

"Don't be silly!"

"She's already said I could have his books when he goes! If that isn't an intimate gesture I don't know what is!"

"I think it's the bottle talking now –You must have had a good quarter of it before you arrived!"

"You drive me to it Allison! Either you or Mrs Parkfield, I don't know.."

"You <u>don't</u> know, you're drunk! Thirty five and over the top! You should be in your prime now Walter. As for Mrs Parkfield –You should be so lucky! She's had her sights on old Bulcastle ever since his wife died."

Walter gets up somewhat unsteadily on his feet and struggles out of the Wendy House.

"I m-must go to the loo...Perhaps I'll have b-better luck there!"

"Mind how you go Walter and don't accept any lifts from strangers!"

He doubles back unsteadily, temporarily.

"Y-Y-You just get back to y-your b-books young Allison Prestatyn! I'm only sorry I c-can't mark yours!" He exits, singing –"'Ding Dong Merrily On High! Glo-ri-a in excel-sis!'"

Some minutes elapse and Allison drinks and marks alternately, John Julian Childs arrives with hat and coat on. He tiptoes up and carols sings at the back window of the Wendy House "'Good King Wenceslas last looked out on the Feast of Stephen' and then pokes his head cheekily through the window:

"Can a strange man offer you some Christmas sweeties

and give you a lift in his reindeer car? I know I'm not as exciting as the 'Danger Stranger' but I'll do my best to oblige!"

"Oh give over John Julian, I want to finish marking these books!"

"Pull the other leg, it's got Christmas bells on!"

"Honestly 'Mr Childs', I'd like to get things finished before the Christmas festivities begin!"

John Julian gallops reindeer-style round to the front and into the Wendy House.

"Looks as though they already have begun! Secret drinking in the Wendy House eh? Mind if I join you?" He sits down and takes the bottle and glasses and pours for both, "Just what the doctor ordered!" They both take a gulp, "It's the only cure for education Allison, when you get to my age!"

"Ooh you're not old John Julian –I know that!"

"I didn't mean that darling –stop reading between the lines on my face!"

"We can't go on meeting like this!..."

"Now that's a cliché if I ever heard one!"

"People are going to start talking! Bob Dredge is already winking and nodding everytime he sees me here after school. Even Walter found me here just now. Didn't you see him in the corridor?"

"Yes, lost his way! Asked me to show him where the gents' toilets were. I pointed him in the right direction. Clever lad Walter! But no sense of direction!"

"He's lovely!"

"You never say things like that about me!"

"All the time, but you never listen. Has Howard Bulcastle been keeping you behind again?"

"Jesus! That man! He's such a bore! There ought to be

capital punishment for Heads who go soldiering on long after the call of early retirement. We sat there with these stock lists and he called out the numbers for me to check and <u>he</u> checked them as well. All afternoon this went on for, and the he sent me round <u>three times</u> –first with the notice about Mrs Teasdale's leaving present, then again with a reminder about Record Books, and yet again with that bit of nonsense about that idiotic seminar <u>on</u> language <u>for</u> language teachers <u>in</u> a language situation etc etc. My God! I'm the highest paid messenger boy in the Borough of Barnside –and this is the sum total of my life after thirty five years teaching!"

"I'd like to go on that language course."

"Everybody's going on courses these days. It's a wonder there's anyone left to teach in the schools. It's not as though the courses are worth going on either. You know, I had to go on one last month as Bulcastle's representative. There were at least twenty head teachers sitting around reading the scripted conversation of two five year old children discussing how to build a castle. Then after lunchbreak we were treated to a video of this great drama! At the end, the lecturer – a slip of a gal no older than you-asked if we had any points to raise. I asked why the children weren't told what a castle <u>was</u> to start with, why they weren't told how to build it properly, and why we all had to waste valuable teaching time sitting around discussing the fact. There was a stunned silence and then they all fell on me with a welter of educational jargon and abuse that quite unnerved me. I was glad to get back to school and the relative sanity of the staffroom!"

"Never mind the staffroom what about the <u>classroom</u>? What about the kids? They love you you know and you didn't even bother to turn up for the special Christmas 'Kids' Disco' last Saturday, after they made that special life-size invitation for you."

"That was Avis's art work! She always likes people to think the kids have done her little creative efforts! Anyway I'm past it as far as discos are concerned."

"It was fun dancing with the kids – they love you to join in!"

"What? Dancing with ten year old maggots? If they love me, which I very much doubt and don't care about anyway, it's because they know I treat them like children and not half-baked adults! I don't believe in child-centred education Allison! Lady Plowden has a lot to answer for! <u>They</u> know that <u>I</u> know that school is a completely unreal situation and I don't take it seriously."

"Avis Gunn wouldn't like to hear you say that!"

"Avis Gunn, God bless her, lives for school and there isn't anything else in her life and I feel truly sorry for her. She's been on more courses than you and I have had hot dinners, and she's extremely busy <u>all</u> the time with school work –she does worksheets and planning schedules until long after the cows come home! When she dies she will go on an eternal course on how to be happy human being –I hope she makes the grade and tells the rest of us what it's like! Oh I must stop this bitching. It's the wine talking now. I didn't know I was capable of drinking so much of Chateau Wendy!"

"What about <u>me</u> then John Julian!"

"What <u>about</u> you? You're young and good looking with the whole of your life in front of you. I hope you have the good sense to grow up and leave this classroom behind you and go out into the big bad dangerous world outside. It's a strange irony that the most successful products of the classroom end up going back to it –Think on that my darling! –I must go!"

"No wait, I hear someone coming!"

They hurriedly close the Wendy House doors. Brenda

enters, carrying a large effigy of an Owl decked in gown and mortarboard.

"Cooee!! Allison are you there? I've brought Wise Owl for you for next term!"

She props it up against the blackboard and stands back admiring her handiwork.

"It was taking up too much space in my activity corner and I always said that you should be the first to benefit from it! ....Are you there? Or must I peep in like a rude little girl!"

There is a sudden moment of realisation of what precisely is going on!

"All right! All right! I know when I'm not wanted!"

She stands defiantly, lights a cigarette and draws on it, arms clasped.

"...And I did want those 'Thelma Hopkins –Hop-on-a-Word' drawing books you <u>promised</u> me! Never mind!"

She exits. The distant choir still rehearse 'Away in a Manger'. There is a few seconds pause and they throw open the Wendy House doors, laughing.

They embrace and John Julian pours another round. They drink and the silence is broken by John Julian:

"I can just see the headlines in next week's 'Barnside Monitor':-

'DEPUTY HEAD DRUNK IN CHARGE OF INFANT TEACHER IN WENDY HOUSE' –She's bound to tell everyone. Good old Brenda!"

"My God, I don't know how I'm going to face her tomorrow. Thank God it's the last day of term!"

They embrace again and at the same time close the Wendy House doors around them. The last verse of 'Away in A Manger' can just be heard. Brenda returns carrying Avis's 'Cuckoo Clock' and she listens intently at the Wendy House doors.

John Julian, drunkenly, "I know! Let's sing 'The Holly and the Ivy'. It's my favourite carol...'The Holly and the Ivy, when they are both full grown of all the trees that are in the wood, the holly bears the crown...'"

Allison starts to join in tunelessly and then starts to giggle uncontrollably. Brenda cries out in anguish, "I've brought you Avis's 'Cuckoo Clock' Allison!....IF YOU CAN SPARE A MOMENT!!" At this sudden desperate cry, all singing stops, "You always wanted it!!"

She flings it on the floor and storms out. The cuckoo mechanism whirrs and wheezes, repeating over and over again –'Cuckoo! Cuckoo! Cuckoo!'

Walter comes upon the scene:

"Hello! Hello! Hello! Who's been upsetting Brenda then?" He picks up the cuckoo clock, "It's stopped! I think it's dead!"

He takes off his party hat in mock reverence.

John Julian is the first to speak after some moments of silence.

"Go away Walter please! And take that bloody cuckoo clock with you <u>and</u> Wise Owl! See you tomorrow!"

"Ch-charming! And c-can I have my b-bottle back please!?"

Allison replies, "I-I'm afraid it's empty! A very Merry Christmas to you Walter and goodnight!"

"...And the same to you Miss P-Prestatyn! Goodnight!" he totters out looking bewildered.

"Heh Walter! I think I've found Mrs Teasdale's gerbil!"

Walter turns, taking his hat off, "Have you indeed! Well s-s-see if you can find one for me Mr Ch-Childs!"

Once again the cuckoo clock really ought to have gone off. Damn!

INTERLUDE 11

OH WHAT A WAY TO GO!

"At last! Free at last! Guess who's pleased!"

The Final Assembly

The Old Hall is as before but decorated with Christmas fripperies –and a Christmas tree with lights stands in one corner. The staff are arrayed on the stage in exactly the same positions as they were on a previous assembly that we took a peep at. They are wearing gaudy gold crown paper hats in jaunty contrast with their wan, exhausted visages. Behind the stage is a heavy velvet closed curtain covering the large mural, that was commissioned from Radcliffe Ball, to set the seal, so to speak, on Mrs Teasdale's valedictory 'Send Jesus to Africa' appeal.

Howard opens proceedings, "Boys and girls this is our final assembly before we break up for Christmas. We have to say our goodbyes too, as Mrs Teasdale is leaving the rough seas of education for the quieter waters of Morecambe Bay –but not before she sends Jesus to Africa with £574-39 in his pocket! Well done Mrs Teasdale (staff wince). So let's start our final assembly off with a bang! (staff wince again). Our final hymn is the school carol especially composed by our resident composer and Deputy Head, Mr Childs!"

Mr Childs duly winces and inappropriately loud cheers ring out which are instantly silenced by Howard Bulcastle.

......"and performed on the pianoforte by our resident concert pianist Miss Hilary Trumble!..."

Howard really is in a good witty mood as it's end of term.

Inappropriately loud cheering is once again instantly silenced.

".....Mr Sidebrother, the projector if you please! Mrs Trumble, the music!"

Hilary gives her usual virtuosic introduction to a conventional hymn tune but with the added genius of Mr Childs' lyrics:

1.   'Let Belle View bells appeal
       As Christian children kneel
       To Mighty God
       Our feet do plod
       Whene'er we seek a meal.

2.   When Christ was born that day
       We saw him in the hay
       A little boy
       Without a toy
       Like us, with feet of clay
          (Repeat 1st verse)

3.   Let Christ come down to see
       Our Belle View School for free
       With constant hearts
       We play our parts
       And try to hide from Thee
          (Repeat 1st verse)

Howard Bulcastle, in full flight, "Get out Bexworth <u>and</u> the boys standing on either side of you! Let us pray. Thank you Lord for helping us to survive this term. Give us, we pray, the strength to come back again to face the perils of a new term. Amen. Get out Johnson! Yes, <u>you</u> Johnson! I would now like to call upon Mrs Teasdale to make her farewell address!....."

Perdita looks frantic as she expected to be called upon to make a presentation on behalf of the staff at this juncture.

"......I give you Mrs Teasdale!......"

Perdita rushes forward to whisper in Mr Bulcastle's ear.

"........Oh sorry! As you were. First, I give you Miss O'Toole instead!"

General all round wincing at this point.

"Thank you Mr Bulcastle. I don't want to bore everyone for too long. I just wanted to say that it is my pleasure to make a presentation to Mrs Teasdale from all the staff in recognition of all those years of devoted service to our school......."

She, somewhat clumsily and with embarrassment, hands over a brown envelope containing a cheque which Mrs Teasdale eagerly opens ands scrutinises.

".......May I say, in passing, Mrs Teasdale that you have done a lot to send Jesus to Africa –May I humbly hope and pray that He comes back soon because we have great need of Him here as well!"

"Thank you Miss O'Toole, you're so right! Thank you children and staff. But let us remember what we are here for. Teachers may come and teachers may go but God goes on forever! I want to thank you from the bottom of my heart for this little gift of yours which will certainly send me all the way to Morecambe Bay, first class but not return. But I also want to thank you for the special gift of £574-39 which will, as Mr Bulcastle said in his inimitable way, send Jesus to Africa with money in his pocket! It is all very well for some to sneer at money. But spiritual things need a bank account to look after them in this wicked world. To save your souls, children, you need to save money –there's no two ways about it!

Now. I've got a special treat for you all. As a constant

reminder of the good that our 'Send Jesus to Africa' Appeal is doing, I commissioned a mural from Mrs Ball which Mr Bulcastle very kindly allowed her to paint on the back wall of our school stage...."

She points to the back, the teachers half turn and the children murmur until instantly quietened by Howard Bulcastle.

"....You may all wonder what a mural is children! Well, I had often wondered myself until, like a good scholar, I looked it up in my dictionary. It's a wall painting. In just a second I'm going to ask Mr Bulcastle to pull the curtain back to show you the painting that Mrs Ball has spent so many weary hours on, when I was taking her Pottery classes three times a week! I don't even know what it looks like myself! It's going to be just as big a surprise to me children as it will be to you! Mr Bulcastle, if you'd be so kind?"

He pulls the curtain back to reveal a huge cartoon-style fresco of a strong-looking bearded, leering pale Jesus, bending down suggestively with his muscular arms round a very slim, nubile young black girl who looks innocently up at him. The 'scrolled' caption reads –'SUFFER LITTLE CHILDREN' to which someone has obviously added in a convenient space underneath 'FORKIN' GRAIRTE MARN' (Afro-Caribbean for 'fucking great man!'). At this climactic moment there is a stunned silence. Mrs Teasdale has obviously not taken in the full significance of what her eyes have taken in.

".....My goodness! It's very nice Mrs Ball! You've obviously put a lot of hard work into it!...."

She puts on her glasses to read out loud what it says.

"....'Suffer the little children'..How apt for a school!... But those last few words! They're African aren't they? They must be the original Swahili words! Oh how like you to be so clever Radcliffe Ball!.."

She attempts to read them without comprehension but with perfect pronunciation!

"...Forkin' grairte Marn!.."

A brief sniggering from the auditorium breaks the deathly silence. With a quick grotesque little movement Mrs Teasdale wheels round, takes off her spectacles and stares at the children in horrified, mute recognition of the truth –her jaw trembling. The Overhead Projector blows up with much noise and smoke, providing all with a merciful diversion. Walter Sidebrother faints. Brenda laughs loudly and hysterically. John Julian covers his face with his hands. The others stare at the mural in vacant astonishment. Avis Gunn's 'Cuckoo Clock' does <u>not</u> burst into life.

FUNERAL GAMES!

In the staffroom days later there is a very different atmosphere. The staff sit around in sombre mood as they await the funeral cars. They are all dressed in black except for Walter who wears a black armband. Brunhilde enters wearing a spectacular Ascot-style black hat and announces:

"Mr Bulcastle your car has arrived. Mr Dredge is taking the flowers in his van if you..." (she breaks down) "..I've known her for nearly twenty years!" She take out a large lacy hankie and blows a trumpet through it.

Bulcastle tries to take command:

"All right! All right! Thank you Miss Waizmann!" she exits, "This is all most embarrassing! Just one more day! Just one more day and she...!" He exits shaking his head.

Brenda, chain-smoking and furious, "...and she would have died on her own patch instead of on his!"

Perdita challenges, "Mrs Gratten, have you no shred of decency?"

"No, thank goodness! Oh grow up Perdita! I've never heard such hypocrisy in all my life! All Howard Bulcastle is concerned about is that she had her fatal heart attack on school premises instead of saving it for the holidays and now he's got to face an official enquiry!" She exhales clouds of smoke. Radcliffe intervenes, "I think you're very rude Brenda. Yes, she did die on school premises and the burden of guilt lies on us all, rightly or wrongly!" Perdita clarifies, "Whoever wrote those disgusting words under your lovely picture, Radcliffe, is the guilty party! I'm not bearing anyone else's guilt but my own. Whoever wrote that filth –Let <u>him</u> stand forward!"

John Julian defends the male sex, "Oh it's a '<u>him</u>' Perdita! That sounds a little like prejudice unless you've got inside information, in which case we all ought to know!.... Come on, spill the beans!"

Perdita snaps back, "I can't imagine any woman writing such filth!"

Brenda, not to be outdone, "Oh come on Perdita! I could, use your imagination!"

Perdita turns on her, "Are you saying then that you did it, Mrs Gratten?"

"I wished I had!"

Hilary responds in surprise, "Oh no Brenda, you can't wish that surely?"

"Oh yes I can. That self-righteous old cow had it coming to her!"

Walter relieves the tension, "How did she actually g-g-go? Was it established that she had a heart at-t-tack?"

Brenda cackles, "Do we have to spell it out for him? She rose bodily in the air and was carried up by a choir of angels dear!"

Allison joins in, "Well, I don't know how she died either. Does anyone know the facts?"

Radcliffe enlightens, "She had a double stroke. Apparently, it was a simultaneous cerebral and coronary attack –quite rare I understand. But it must have been brought on by the shock of seeing those words under my mural."

John Julian, relishing the occasion, "Well, she certainly went in style. If she didn't have the heavenly choir, she certainly had the earthly one courtesy of Belle View 4th Years! ..I expect when I go it will be quite unceremonious... the trail of chalk on the board...the kids huddled round the Slumped body...Little Terry Phillips telling his mates that now they needn't do the homework I set them!"

Avis Gunn rushes in late, looking flushed and carrying a blackboard and easel under her arm.

"Oh thank goodness you haven't gone yet. Sorry I'm late everyone.."

She puts down her blackboard and easel, "....I was just clearing her room!" Brenda, aghast, "Got in quick didn't we Avis? Body hardly cold in the earth etc etc?"

"Brenda Gratten shame on you! One of her last requests was that I should clear her room, and she did say that I could have anything that could be useful to my classroom!"

"...Oh, all that with her dying breath was it Avis?"

Allison, also aghast, "Miss Gunn, you simply can't have all that stock. She promised Hilary and I her tacki-back rolls and the art equipment was to go to Radcliffe and Perdita was to have the paper, books and pencils!"

"This is the first I've heard of it! Mr Bulcastle himself

is a witness, she distinctly said to me that the 'Gay Musical Weather Elephant' was to come to me as well as all the easels and paints! You ask him!"

Perdita outrages, "I'm sorry Miss Gunn, I really must support Allison here. I'm sure that she wouldn't be so mean as to give all her stock to just one person. It would be so unlike her to do a thing like that!"

We have a veritable chorus of response at this point with everyone talking at once:

Avis pleads, "But she quite definitely promised me these things!"

Allison justifies, "It's only fair to share what there is Avis –it is school stock!"

Hilary decides, "Howard Bulcastle ought to decide this once and for all!" Radcliffe confirms, "Isn't that what I have been saying all along? It's not our decision!"

John Julian humorously placates, "Spoils of war in the blackboard jungle –to mix my metaphors! Can't we stop behaving like educational vultures just for once!! Where are those cars??"

He gets up and impatiently looks out of the staffroom window. There is silence for a few seconds. Brunhilde enters again reading from a list:

"The cars have arrived for Miss O'Toole, Miss Ball, Miss Prestatyn, Mrs Trumble and Miss Grimes!" They promptly depart. Only John Julian, Walter and Brenda Gratten remain.

John Julian reflects, "Miss Grimes has gone on. I wonder why we three are the last Brenda?"

"The family have their suspicions dear!" Brenda cackles.

Walter interjects, "Avis is wrong you know Mr Childs. When she was 'to come into her kingdom', as she put it, I was to have the 'Wendy House', the big one in the Infant Hall."

"..And I hope you will be very happy in it dear, that's all I can say!" Brenda cackles.

"Don't you worry Walter. You'll get your 'Wendy House', if I've got anything to do with it. I dread to think what she's left me (to Brenda) Fancy a ciggie?" She accepts the proffered cigarette.

"Probably her white leatherbound school bible dear! She probably thinks you need it!" She cackles as she lights up.

"I don't know what I need Brenda, that's my trouble!"

"And I know what I need and that's mine dear –What do you need -Walter?"

"Her big 'Wendy House' of course! (Brenda cackles) and I <u>would</u> like my play to be put on as soon as p-p-possible! Those are my only pressing needs at present!"

Brenda, drawing on her cigarette, inhaling and exhaling tusks of smoke, "Lucky you! But I thought Bulcastle had dropped your play on account of recent happenings? He told me that there was enough drama in the school at present without adding to it!" She cackles again.

"No it's only going to be postponed until the first week of next term and then all will be revealed -eh Walter?"

"That's right Mr Ch-Childs....I-I-I still can't g-g-get the ending right but it'll probably be all right on the night!"

"I wish I could get my orgasms through plays or art or craft or needlework – or anything!" She titters almost to the point of tears.

Brunhilde enters once again, like a herald, to pronounce from her list:

"Your car Mrs Gratten! You travel with the infant staff!" she exits brusquely.

"Now that's what I need, a good funeral!" she cackles as she leaves. John Julian offers Walter a cigarette.

"Oh I forgot, you don't smoke! (he lights his own from

the butt of the last one.) We're the last. It must mean we're under suspicion Walter lad.

They think that, either you or I or both of us, constitute the deus ex machina of this sordid little comedy or is it a tragedy –I'm still trying to make up my mind. I reckon your little play will provide all the clues for us Walter and then we'll know it was you who dunnit!"

"D-Don't be ridiculous! It isn't finished yet, I told you!"

"Well, I wasn't the one who wrote those fateful words I can tell you! My sentiments but not my words! I'm much too much of a coward to do anything like that. It <u>must</u> have been you Walter! You never liked her much did you? She was always <u>preying</u> on you, in more ways than one! Well? It was you, wasn't it?"

Brunhilde bursts in again.

"Our car Walter. Mr Childs you'll be following in the last car with Mr Peasanthwartes and the people from the education offices. I think Howard wants you to sweeten them up a bit. He's afraid of 'repercussions' over this very sad business!"

She gets out a large lace handkerchief, especially embroidered for such occasions, and sobs and snuffles into it as she and Walter exit.

John Julian sits and broods for a while and then makes as though to search his pockets for more cigarettes. He brings out a silvery object that looks like a gun –actually it's the school starting pistol that has been left in his black suede jacket since the previous Sports' Day –a little wry amusement here as he he puts the pistol to his temple in a mock gesture of suicide.

At this point Betty Teasdale enters!

The readers will not be expecting this as they will have assumed that she was the one who died of a stroke at the unveiling ceremony. Actually, the one who died was Mrs Hunningford a colleague and close friend of Betty's.

"I hope I'm not too late!.......Goodness! What <u>are</u> you doing? You cowardly wretch! I might have guessed that you'd take the easy way out John Julian Childs! And it's taken the untimely death of Griselda Hunningford to make you feel remorse at last has it? (Going to the kettle) I must have a coffee. So it was you who wrote those vile words –of course. I hope I haven't missed the funeral car."

John Julian, laughing contemptuously, "I like the way you mix up your snide little references with mundane observations and casual small talk. It's a clever little trick that you've practised over the years Betty to make your malice more palatable. Everyone falls for it except for me!"

Betty pouring out the coffee, "Why don't you pull the trigger John Julian if it makes you feel any better! Or would you prefer a coffee instead?

"Ooh no Betty, I'll pull that trigger I think (silence)..... It's only the school starting pistol you know –I must have left it in my jacket pocket. I haven't worn this jacket since Sports' Day."

Betty whimpering, "I've known Griselda Hunningford for the best part of thirty years –that it should come to this! How you can sit there and joke and make your fake gestures just shows how shallow you really are!! Those disgusting words under Radcliffe's picture killed her just as surely as a gun fired against her temple would have done!"

"Oh don't be so melodramatic Betty! We all knew she was terminally ill – she could have gone at any moment, it was common knowledge. Howard Bulcastle was hoping she'd finally drop dead after the end of term to spare him the embarrassment of dealing with it. Unfortunately God couldn't oblige!"

"You're a wicked man John Julian Childs! Callous!"

"No Betty. I don't think I'm wicked or callous. They're much too full-blooded as adjectives to apply to me. I think I can best be described as detached, unhappily so perhaps, and my limited knowledge of theology tells me that this isn't exactly a sin as I can't really help it you know!"

Betty, bringing over his coffee, "Haven't you heard of sins of omission?" John Julian, daydreaming, "What?"

"Yes, you are detached aren't you! You think you're so superior to everybody else!! I've often wondered someone as superior as you should have ended up in a primary school! Of course, men in primary schools tend to be a poor lot as men, odd balls, failures of one sort and another...But you, you could have done a lot of things....You know what I think? I think you're a moral coward! I think you've taken refuge from the real adult world where people have to make painful, costly decisions about good and evil, life and death. You're hiding in a 'Wendy House' John Julian and you know it and it hurts!! What's that word the children use a lot these days. 'sussed' yes, 'sussed'. I've sussed you out at last John Julian Childs!!"

He points the gun at her and pulls the trigger. Betty looks surprised, gives a little shriek and drops the cup. Then the gun goes off with a deafening report. Betty drops down stone dead of heart failure.

John Julian is stunned. He looks down at her for a few seconds:

"Betty? Oh come on now! It's just a starting pistol, it must have had a blank still in it. It's quite harmless really. Just a toy gun. The children fiddle around with it in science lessons –they're always leaving the catch off!"

He kneels down to examine her. He gets flustered and angry:

"Betty!! I was just-just indulging in one of those 'Wendy House' whimsies that Walter so heartily approves of –I bet he's got a scene like this in his play.....Betty please!! This is ridiculous –it's a farce! This isn't the way it should end, No one will swallow this Betty!! Betty?? It's too contrived, it just won't work...Oh dear! Oh dear!! What to do!"

At this point one of the chauffeurs of the funeral cars comes along. He just puts his head round the staffroom door and doesn't actually see what has happened.

"The funeral car is waiting sir –The car for Barnfield Crematorium –Are you ready sir?"

"Yes, yes, as ready as I'll ever be anyway! (Chauffeur closes the door and goes)....'Are you ready for the funeral car?'..(he chuckles)..Betty it's a classic line! This must be the end of Walter's play!! Betty?? Betty??"

INTERLUDE 12

DOES JOHN JULIAN GET
THE LAST WORD?

IT ISN'T BELIEVABLE IS IT? THE SCENES DON'T LAST long enough —not enough development of plot or character, too many people anyway! <u>And</u> he spoils it all with those awful educational diatribes sandwiched awkwardly in the middle of real scenes —then there are those pathetic little devices of the 'cuckoo clock' and the Overhead Projector noisily interfering where there should be some proper continuity....Mind you, between you and me and the blackboard, I got some quiet satisfaction out of seeing Betty Teasdale get her come-uppance. She always was the incarnation of the deity at Belle View School and I always wanted to commit deicide.....Brenda Gratten was quite nicely sketched out. She is affectionately known as 'the scourge of Belle View'. Every time you meet her you have to reach for your tin of Elastoplast. There isn't a single member of staff who hasn't felt the lash of her tongue...Walter rather courageously got himself right...But he chickened our in the end. Old 'Scaredy Cat' would not admit who really put Betty down! You see, he's still frightened of her. The ghost of Betty Teasdale walks yet. Yes, I have to admit the characters are absolutely right.

The dialogue is quite clever at times...But there's something missing from the story —a lack of... a lack of real narrative tension, a lack of development of character. In truth, it's a 'Wendy House' story! And maybe that's just the point....But let me finish with a little confession —the author's going to love me for saying this!....Actually, I was the one who wrote those rude words under Radcliffe's mural... Puerile as it all now seems!...I did it miss, honest I did! And what's more, I'm glad I did!"

POSTSCRIPT

John Julian didn't get the Last Word!

A T AROUND 5.30PM ON JANUARY 11TH 1985, MR JOHN Julian Childs, Deputy Head Teacher of Belle View Primary School, was making his way across the school playground to the Car Park. He was just about to get into his car when he was accosted by a fellow teacher, a Mrs Brenda Gratten. There was an exchange of words followed by screaming. Mr Childs fell to the ground with stab wounds to the chest from which he later died in hospital.

There were several eye witnesses to the tragic occurrence.

Mr Dredge, the school caretaker said, "I was just emptying the rubbish baskets when I heard loud voices and a woman's scream. I ran over to find Mr Childs lying face down and Mrs Gratten standing over him with a kitchen knife in her hand. There was blood everywhere!"

Mr Bulcastle, the Head teacher of Belle View School, said, "I don't know what to say. I've known both the teachers concerned for fifteen years or more..I was just getting into my car as Mr Childs was getting into his. Then all of a sudden Mrs Gratten rushes up and screams at him and she just starts stabbing him in the chest...I tried to restrain her but it was too late! That's three deaths (indicating with his fingers) in our school in the space of a week, I'm sorry I can't cope!"

Miss Allison Prestatyn, an Infant teacher at the school, said, "I can't talk about it –I saw it all. She just wouldn't take no for an answer –she had it in for him ever since I came to the school. She was a jealous harridan, she hated him!..I'm too upset to talk anymore, I'm sorry!"

Mr Walter Sidebrother, a Junior teacher at the school, said, "I was getting a lift from Mr Childs and I was waiting at his car. Just as Mr Childs arrives, Mrs Gratten suddenly runs up and starts shouting at him.

She said something like '..A nice, clean meaningful,

artistic death, is that what you wanted John Julian? How about a bit of reality eh? Eh?'.

Then she produced a bread knife and she said. 'You didn't expect to find this in your 'Wendy House' did you?' Immediately she lunged at him and stabbed him several times in the chest..It was awful..He didn't even resist!.. He just looked surprised and stared at the blood spurting out of his chest and then stared back at her and his mouth kept opening and closing as though he was trying to say something and then he staggered forward in the direction of the school, looked up at it with his eyes rolling and fell flat on his face..I couldn't do anything..I was paralysed! Then Mr Bulcastle kind of held Mrs Gratten back and Mr Dredge shook her arm and she dropped the knife...Allison was there as well and she was crying bitterly..It was awful!!"

EPILOGUE

We Can Only Dream!

B UT THEY WILL NEVER DIE. AVIS IS FLAPPING AROUND in that great orderly classroom in the sky with Radcliffe in attendance, taking care of her when necessary. Hilary is still there, gate-crashing heavenly assemblies with her virtuosity and verbosity. There is a 'No Smoking' sign in paradise but Brenda, waiting in the shadows, ignores it and broods for all eternity. Perdita is knitting scarves for the angels and loudly condemning the keepers of the pearly gates. Bob Dredge is forever making an earnestly reasoned complaint about the ultimate safety hazard from which there is no known legislative cure –death! Allison glows in wonder at the stars as innocent as life itself. Howard Bulcastle is satisfied with the arrangements as meticulously detailed out to him by a beaming Brunhilde Waizmann. Walter is excited about a new subject now for the play that will never be written. Betty Teasdale armed with the sword of self-righteousness hunts down the undeserving for ever and ever. Amen.

Only the shade of John Julian Childs remains restless, searching in vain for the 'nice, clean, meaningful, artistic' end to his story.........